EARTH

The Elemental Series, Book One

by

Nicki Greenwood

Earth: The Elemental Series, Book One

COPYRIGHT © 2009 by Nicki Greenwood

Cover Art by *Kim Mendoza*

The Wild Rose Press
PO Box 708
Adams Basin, NY 14410-0706
Visit us at www.thewildrosepress.com

Publishing History
First Faery Rose Edition, 2010
Print ISBN 1-60154-675-0

Published in the United States of America

Kincade swept a hand at the barren ground of the trail. "This look like a good enough spot to stop for more soil samples?"

"Sure," Ally answered, dragging her gaze away from him with a pang of regret.

They slipped from their horses together. Cade led his mount to the edge of the worn dirt trail and tied its reins to a sturdy branch. He turned back to take her horse's reins as she led the animal closer. The motion brought him up short just inches away.

His body went rigid as stone. Time stopped and held its breath with her.

The warmth in her face could have been the sun. The tingle on her skin might have been the light breeze lifting her hair. But only the green, green depths of his eyes caused such a quivering in her belly. Standing mere inches away, he studied her like some ancient mystery.

He loomed close enough for his body heat to draw a sharp contrast to the cool mountain air. His gaze dropped to her mouth. She heard the soft hiss of his indrawn breath, and he took half a step closer. Her heartbeat doubled speed. "We shouldn't do this," he murmured.

For once in her life, she didn't care what she should or shouldn't do. Everything ceased to exist but the phantom heat emanating from him. She took a breath to slow her pounding heart and closed the distance between their bodies. "What if I want to?"

A haunted look flashed across his face. Faint lines formed between his brows. "*I* shouldn't, Ally."

Disappointment speared her. Unwilling to let him see how much his refusal hurt, she turned away.

His warm, rough hand slipped into hers. Surprised, she turned back.

He stepped closer and rooted her to the spot with a heated stare. "I didn't say I didn't want to."

Dedication

This book could not have happened without the love and support of my family, and the family of writers I have gained along the way.

To my family, many hugs and thanks for believing in me. I love you more than you know.

To the amazing members of the Central New York Romance Writers, you rock, and if it were up to me you would all have nonstop bestsellers. Write on!

Chapter One

"What do you mean, you're losing your power?"

The demand echoed in Cade Murphy's ears. He stared across the farmhouse table at his foster brother, who stood rigid beside the apron-front sink. Surprise registered loud and clear on Ethan Sutter's face. "I didn't say I'm losing it," Cade answered.

"You said it isn't working," Ethan said. "That's losing it, in my book."

Cade shoved his breakfast plate away. Bad enough his earth-healing gift had been on the fizzle for the past three weeks, and the ranch's crops looked so awful. He felt like a ticking time bomb about to explode into his foster siblings' lives. They depended on him and he was letting them down. Again.

Maybe, since he'd been accidentally gifted with supernatural ability in the first place, he wasn't meant to keep it. That thought did little to ease the sting of failure creeping under his skin.

Snatching up his coffee mug, he examined the dregs in the bottom. "Damn it." A glance toward the coffee pot confirmed it had likewise been drained dry. A lot like he felt these days. "I've written for help."

Ethan plopped into an opposite chair. "You don't tell us you're losing your power, and then you go and contact outside help to fix it? From who, the circus sideshow?"

"I'm not looking for help to fix *me*. Just a little push to get the ranch running right again until my power comes back."

1

"*If* it comes back." Ethan pulled Cade's plate toward himself, then fished in his shirt pocket for a cigarette lighter. He picked up the crust of toast Cade had left uneaten and lit it, then dropped it back onto the plate.

The scent of scorched bread filled the kitchen and stung Cade's nose until his eyes watered. "What the hell are you doing?"

Ethan waved his fingers over the crust. The flame leaped higher, bounced over the bread's surface, then sputtered out. "Checking to see if I still have *my* power."

"I haven't lost it. And it's not contagious," Cade spat, though he didn't know about that last part. He avoided looking at his hands, which he curled around his empty mug.

"How do you know it's not contagious?"

Cade shot his foster brother a warning glare.

As usual, Ethan ignored the look and went on ranting. "Do you have any idea what the girls are going to do with a bunch of strangers getting into our business? You should have asked us first."

"Since when are you the voice of reason?"

Ethan pushed a hand through his wild, rust-red hair. "I'm just worried how they'll take a crowd of people poking around Hope Creek where their noses don't belong."

"Wrong. You're worried about you, like you always are. And it's one nose. Her name is Allyson Hamilton. She's from Montana State's Department of Plant Pathology."

With a mocking snort, Ethan rocked his chair until only the back legs touched the floor. "A plant biologist. Why don't you just invite the Forest Service? They could use you for promotional ads. 'Grow trees, kids, don't burn them.' "

"You're funny," Cade growled, but Ethan's barb bothered him more than he liked to admit. For a man who'd been able to make any plant flourish since age ten when the accident happened, he'd become a dismal asset to Hope Creek. He thumbed the rim of his still-warm coffee mug. "Miss Hamilton's going to be here this afternoon. If you don't want to meet her, I suggest you ride herd in the north pasture."

A broad grin crossed Ethan's stubbled face until his pale hazel eyes flashed. His chair thumped back onto all four legs. "Want her to yourself? She must not be older than dirt, then. So to speak."

Cade sighed. "I don't want her here any more than you do, Ethan, but if she can help us bring in a decent crop this fall, we might have a chance of *not* losing our home. I'm just trying to keep the four of us together the best I can. We're all we've got, powers or no powers."

Ethan managed to look scolded for all of three seconds before surging to his feet. He stalked back toward the kitchen counter, then grabbed his battered cowboy hat off a stack of old seed catalogs. Clapping the hat onto his shaggy head, he added, "Be sure and tell *Miss* Hamilton she's working with a bunch of Elementals. That'll make for nice reading in her final report to her department."

Before Cade could reprimand him again, Ethan slipped out of the kitchen, boots thumping away down the hall. The front door banged shut.

Damn, and damn again.

Cade pulled a crumpled letter from his back pocket and scanned it once more, rubbing his aching forehead with the other hand. Montana State's letterhead clamored for attention at the top of the letter, but his eyes went right to the name at the bottom of the page instead: Allyson Hamilton. The letter proclaimed her a skilled botanist with extensive laboratory experience.

But no real experience, he thought, filling in the

blanks the letter hadn't. And no fancy letters at the end of her name. So either she was still working on her degree, or the department didn't consider him enough bother to send a more qualified staff member. He supposed he shouldn't have been picky, since he wasn't paying for the consultation. Doctor Coonan, the department head, had offered help in exchange for using part of the ranch as a field lab for first-year students.

Ha. Wait until Ethan found that one out. He'd blow a fuse for sure.

With a last, regretful glance at the empty coffee pot, Cade tucked the letter away in his pocket and stood up to start morning chores.

Bracing, pine-scented mountain air teased his nose as he descended the porch steps. He crossed the potholed driveway, dismayed at the thought of another expensive repair. They had yet to rebuild the barn they'd almost lost in a fire last year. That disaster had cost them the best of their horses and nearly spelled the end of Hope Creek. If ever Cade needed his Elemental earth power, it was now, with the bank and his neighbor and business contractors all breathing down his neck to buy the ranch.

The time had come for desperate measures. Only here at Hope Creek had he ever felt free of the watchful, judgmental eyes of the world, and he'd work his hands raw before he lost that solace. God help him—and his foster brother and sisters—if his power didn't return in time to boost the failing pastureland before they went belly-up.

If his power returned at all. Ethan was right.

He pushed open the loading door of the cow barn. It boasted two long rows of stalls, mostly empty since the bulk of the herd was out in the pasture. A barn fan whirred at the far end, siphoning out the already-stuffy air. A few remaining Herefords and one or two Black Angus cows munched on piles of alfalfa in their mangers. A young Hereford mooed as he entered the barn. He gave her neck a pat and went to the tool rack for a pitchfork.

Cleaning stalls and laying down fresh straw proved a welcome distraction to his worries. Soon, he heard a woman's voice call out behind him. "Mister Murphy? Kincade Murphy?"

Wiping his sweaty brow, he laid his pitchfork against a stall divider, then turned toward the open loading door. A curvy, feminine figure stood silhouetted in the light from outside.

Definitely not older than dirt. Some distant, long-ignored part of him perked up in cautious interest. He squashed it back. "Yeah."

The woman came forward, hand outstretched, into the dim barn interior. As she approached, Cade made out flaming red hair and flushed cheeks. "Allyson Hamilton. I'm really sorry, Mister Murphy. I'm afraid my dog's gotten loose."

He closed his hand around hers, raising an eyebrow at the contrast between his suntanned paw and her slender, pale fingers. "Did you say you brought your dog?"

"Yes. I mean, no. I meant to bring him to the kennel after I spoke with you about your ranch. When I opened the door, he saw your horses and took off. I'm really, *really* sorry—"

Hell in a handbasket. If the mutt pestered Diablo, the stallion might kick him clear into the next county. Cade dropped the woman's hand and hurried out of the barn without another word.

In the horse pasture, a pair of chestnut mares kicked up their heels and tossed their heads. A small, brownish-black shape leaped through the grass after them, while Cade's younger foster sister chased after the whole mêlée, calling "Here, boy!" to no avail.

Cade whistled to the woman. "Elsa, get out of there before Diablo comes after you!" He broke into a jog.

Gleeful barking filled the air as he vaulted over the fence. A shining white tail tip poked up like an antenna from the grass, and Cade glimpsed the flap of canine ears. With a swipe, he shooed Elsa back over the fence, then he charged after the dog.

He grabbed for the mutt, but it wriggled out of his reach and plunged after the horses once more. The mares bolted away, stretching the distance between themselves and the elusive dog.

Hoofbeats pounded the earth and a shrill scream pierced the air. Cade saw an enormous black shape from the corner of his eye. "Son of a—"

Diablo, seventeen hands of burly, pissed-off stallion, barreled right at him with pinned ears. The stallion shrilled again, long strides swallowing the ground. Cade darted forward, watching as Diablo bared his teeth and lowered his head. The dog remained blissfully ignorant of its danger.

Lunging, Cade snatched the dog by its scruff. The fuzzy mutt squirmed as he scooped it out of the stallion's reach. Diablo thundered past, trailing a wake of dusty wind behind him. Before the stallion could circle back for another assault, Cade rushed the fence and sailed over it, panting.

He checked his warm, furry prize. A gangly beagle pup, still squirming, this time in an effort to reach his face with its slobbery tongue. The pup's too-long tail whipped his arm in a frantic, joyful rhythm. "You're plumb clueless, mutt," he grumbled.

Allyson gripped a fencepost, looking even paler than she had a moment ago. "Oh, my God. Mister Murphy, I'm so..."

"They do make leashes," he said, pushing the dog into her arms.

For a moment her eyes met his, cloud-gray and

full of censure as if he were the one at fault. "I had one. He broke the clip." She hugged the pup against her face. The dog yipped and slobbered on her instead.

Which, okay, was kind of cute.

Diablo snorted behind them, reminding Cade that *he* had almost been flattened right along with her dog. Clearing his throat, he said, "Elsa, go back to the horse barn. I've got things settled here."

His foster sister gave him her big, blue-eyed, you're-being-mean-to-people look, but retreated back into the horse barn where she'd been doing chores.

"I really am sorry, Mister Murphy," Allyson said into her dog's fur.

"I take it he isn't used to farms."

"Actually, he's very used to them," she replied. Her gaze lifted again, pinning him. "My father's a semi-retired vet. Bailey goes on calls with him every now and then."

"Hopefully on a leash," he said, meeting her stare with a pointed one of his own. Her expression still held a hint of reproach, but her cheeks colored and cautious interest raised its head again. He cleared his throat once more. Damn annoying tickle. "Why don't we get your dog back in the car, and you can tell me what you plan to do to help my pasture?"

And then she smiled. A brilliant, broad, sunny grin that lit her up and hit him like a blow to the solar plexus. "I've got lots of ideas," she said, scratching behind the pup's ears. She started toward a beat-up blue sedan parked in front of the house.

Cade followed as if an invisible thread connected them, thoughts still lingering on her dazzling smile. She seemed so confident, so ready to tackle the problem.

Maybe, just maybe, she could help him get Hope Creek back on track while there was still time to fend off the bill collectors.

****

One week. Doctor Coonan had told Ally she had one week to solve Kincade Murphy's problem. She'd never been given such a protracted deadline, and she suspected Doctor Coonan's new assistant had something to do with that.

Fresh out of college with mediocre grades, Julie Belhurst relied more on her looks than her brains. She'd set her sights on Allyson's job, and didn't mind showing some leg to get her superiors to help her usurp the position. In spite of her hard work, Ally had been pushed back for promotions again and again since Julie's arrival. Meanwhile, Julie enjoyed the petting and praise of the mostly-male department staff.

Let's see her pull off a site evaluation in seven days or less, Ally thought. Then her self-confidence faded. *That's if I can work that fast.*

She pushed her worries to the back of her mind as she and Kincade reached her car. Bailey wriggled in her arms and almost escaped again. She managed to open her car door, set him down, snatch a folder, then shut the door again without him getting away.

When she turned back around, she found Kincade staring into the backseat of her car with what looked like alarm. She followed his gaze to the rumpled pile of clothing, fast food bags, and boxes of science equipment scattered across the seat. "I know it's a mess," she said, trying for a tone of amusement. "My work is a lot more organized than my car."

"Looks to me like you've set up camp in there," he responded. One sable eyebrow lifted over his grass-green eyes.

Bailey whined and shoved his nose into the crack of her rolled-down window. She let him lick her fingers. "My department supervisor mentioned something about you having a bunkhouse."

8

Kincade's eyebrow inched higher. "He did, did he?"

Oops. Ally grimaced. Julie had been the one to deliver the memo on the Murphy project. Apparently, she'd fudged about the sleeping arrangements. What else had she left out? No doubt she intended to sabotage Ally before she'd even started by making her look as unprepared as possible. *Score one for Julie. The little monster's not as stupid as she likes people to think.* "Look, I can find a motel in town," she said, striving to regain her show of confidence.

"She can stay here," interrupted a female voice.

Two women came toward them, one of them the blonde Kincade had earlier referred to as Elsa. The other, tall with chestnut hair, stopped as she reached them. Her vivid blue gaze settled on Ally. "Sagerton's thirty miles away. She'll be driving here and back in pitch dark with no road signs."

Kincade's shoulders stiffened and drew sharp lines under his flannel shirt, but he said nothing.

The brunette fisted a hand on her hip. "Don't tell me you're going to make this poor woman drive all the way to Sagerton and back every day, just to make her sleep in that roach motel they call an inn." As quickly as her anger surfaced, it submerged again. She extended a hand toward Ally. "Morgan Clifton, Cade's foster sister."

Ally shook the woman's hand. "Look, I don't want to put anybody out—"

"You're not," Cade said at last. "There's a foal-watch bunk in the horse barn."

"That's right," Elsa added. "There's a stove, a fridge, even a shower. Just like a little apartment."

Morgan grinned, and Ally got the feeling the woman had buffaloed her foster brother more than once. "Ethan says Miss Hamilton's here to help improve the pasture," the brunette said to Kincade.

"It's about time you got some sense and hired help."

"Might want to tell Ethan that," Kincade muttered. "He seems to disagree."

"Ethan gets his shorts in a knot every other minute." Morgan slipped an arm around Allyson's shoulders. "And don't worry about your dog. He can stay, too."

Glowering, Kincade straightened to his full height—impressive, since Ally barely reached his chin. "I'm not going to have a dog scaring up the horses. What if he gets kicked next time?"

"Diablo's as much of a grouch as Ethan," Morgan said, waving a hand as if to dismiss the problem. "As long you have him on a leash around the horses, Allyson, everything should work out fine." She glanced at Kincade again. "Elsa and I will be in the house working on dinner. Don't be late."

With that, the women strode away. Ally stared after them, picturing a receding typhoon. What on earth had just happened?

Cheeks burning, she raised her gaze to Kincade's. "I can find other arrangements if it bothers you to have me stay."

He opened his mouth as if to say something, then snapped it shut again. His gaze slid back to her car, where Bailey struggled to jam more than his nose into the crack of her open window. "Is he housebroken?"

"Yeah. He's a really good boy, most of the—"

"Just keep him away from the horses. I'll show you to your bunk." He stalked toward the horse barn without waiting to see if she followed.

Not much for smiling, was he? Well, he didn't have to like her—just let her do her job. Determined to show her professionalism, she jogged after him. Her stare landed on his sable-dark hair, then trailed down over his broad back and skimmed lean, muscular limbs that suggested a lot of hard ranch work.

Why, then, she wondered, *does he need me?* From what she'd gathered so far, he had plenty of help around here to keep the ranch working. Heavy metals in the soil? Not likely, or his problem would have occurred long before now. Overuse of the land? Maybe, but Kincade didn't look the type to be irresponsible about grazing his animals.

Sabotage from a competing ranch?

She scoffed at her overactive imagination. She'd been watching too many crime shows lately, looking for angles where none existed.

She followed him down the breezeway until they stopped at a plank door with a wrought iron latch. He pushed open the door to reveal a cozy little hideaway.

The twin pine bed had been draped in plaid wool blankets. At its foot rested a large steamer trunk. Paintings of horses adorned the knotty pine walls, and a beam of sunlight filtered in through the gingham-curtained window. In the opposite corner, she saw a small desk, an efficiency kitchen, and the doorway to what must have been the bathroom. "This is prettier than my apartment in the city," she said, entering the room ahead of him. She laid a hand on a smooth-sanded bedframe post. "I'll feel like I'm on vacation."

Kincade's stern features left no clue to his thoughts. "Elsa keeps it stocked with soap and whatnot. If you need anything else, you can ask her." He turned toward the door.

Why was he in such a hurry to get away from her? He'd been the one to ask for her help, after all. "How long before dinner?" she called. "I'd like to start right away by taking some soil samples and sending them back to the lab."

The first glimmer of warmth—or was it approval?—flared in his evergreen eyes, and her stomach pitched. Unbidden, curiosity swelled within her about what his smile must be like, when a mere look could produce such a reaction.

He seemed not to notice her agitation. "I'll walk you around the place after we eat," he said. "You can keep your dog in one of the empty stalls while we do that."

On the way back out to her car to get her things, Ally spotted a partly-collapsed building past the cow barn. Some of the beams were new, and others bore ugly black soot marks. "What happened there?"

He kept walking. "Barn fire last year. We're rebuilding."

"Was it very bad?" she pressed, her mind spinning with images of flames roaring into the sky. Nothing less than a four-alarm fire could have left the building in such a wreck.

"Bad enough."

He gave no further comment while they finished putting her suitcases and gear into her new quarters. After that he led her back to the cow barn.

Scanning the interior, she nibbled at her lower lip. When she caught him watching, green eyes aglow in the dim light, she stopped at once. A tiny shiver swept down her back as he held her with that mystifying stare. Did he somehow think the answers to his problems were written on her face?

Needing to break the tension, she scooped a residual handful of alfalfa from the closest manger. "Do you grow your own feed?"

He grunted. "Couldn't afford not to. Prices around here aren't exactly low."

"Not dusty." She sniffed it for the musty odor of mildew, but only the scent of sun-dried grasses filled her nostrils.

Standing up straight, he said, "I wouldn't give my stock bad feed."

"I'm not suggesting that. Could I see a full bale?"

With a shrug, he led her out of the cow barn to a shed nearby. She thrust an arm into the nearest bale and pulled out a small fistful of hay. "Is this a last cutting?"

"First cutting last season," he said.

She raised her brows. He must have been in dire straits longer than the couple of weeks Doctor Coonan's memo had indicated, if last season's forage looked this bad. She sniffed the handful, rubbed it between her fingers, then sprinkled it back on the bale. "Do you use fertilizers?"

"Nothing the cows don't already produce by themselves." A single shallow dimple appeared in his unshaven cheek.

So he did smile...a little. Her insides jumped and she had to refocus on the bales of hay stacked in the shed. "You might improve your forage if you use some other kinds," she suggested.

His smile evaporated at once. "I don't use chemicals on my land."

"There are any number of fertilizers that are perfectly safe when used properly—"

"And that's fine for other ranches," he interrupted, "but not mine."

"I haven't tested it yet, but your soil may be lacking some vital nutrients."

"No means no, Miss Hamilton."

A faint clanging roused her from her puzzlement over his refusal. "That would be dinner," he announced, stepping away from the door and holding out his arm as if to let her lead the way.

She hesitated, then started forward at the same time as he did. Both of them halted, bottlenecked in the narrow doorframe, chest-to-chest. Or, rather, nose-to-chest. Nose to very *broad* chest.

Flame poured into her cheeks. Lord, she must look like a redheaded tomato. "Ah, excuse me... My foot. It's stuck..." She lifted her tennis shoe, but he'd trapped the trailing lace under the sole of his boot.

She raised her stare from his well-defined chest and met his blazing emerald eyes. Something stirred within their depths and it seemed that suddenly, everything around them disappeared. His eyes drew her in as though she had slipped into some vast, timeless forest, full of birdsong and the scent of green, growing things. Mesmerized, she sucked in a gasp of air. Gooseflesh sprang up along her arms.

His eyes widened, fixing on hers with startling intensity. His lips parted and his breath fanned her face. The earlier jolt in her belly multiplied into a thundering brass band. She lost herself in his primal stare.

Until he turned away. He lifted his boot, freeing her shoelace, and slipped past her out the door, leaving her breathless.

Apparently, no matter how much Kincade Murphy wanted it to, no didn't strictly mean no.

Chapter Two

Cade sat at the long farmhouse table and breathed in the aroma of mesquite-grilled steak. Elsa set a steaming platter of fresh corn in the middle of the table, then sat beside him in her customary seat.

Across the table, Ally studied the heaps of food. In addition to the steak and corn, his sisters had laid out a basket of rolls, a bowl of salad, and baked potatoes. Ally turned to Morgan, who sat at one end of the table. "Are you expecting more company?"

"We cook a big meal on weekends," Morgan explained. "The rest of the week, it's easier for us to pack leftovers and head out to do chores. If you get hungry later, grab something from the fridge. Don't be shy."

"I can't imagine getting hungry again after all of this." Ally laughed.

The sound stirred the interest Cade had been trying to ignore since the incident in the hay shed. No, since before that. *It'll go away,* he told himself, *as soon as she's been here long enough for the novelty to wear off.*

At least he hoped so. The last time he'd been attracted to a woman, their relationship had ended in a mess that almost blew his foster family's cover. Cade didn't relish the idea of them all being exposed as Elementals and getting forced out of town by fearful witch hunters. Or worse, allowed to stay, but condemned as hocus-pocus-practicing charlatans.

His ex, Maryanne, had done him a favor by steering him away from any further romantic traps.

He'd have thanked her, if he didn't already dislike her too much to talk to her.

Elsa's soft voice broke into his thoughts. "Where's Ethan?"

"Right here," Ethan answered, entering the kitchen. He tugged on a lock of Elsa's hair, then rounded the table to sit down. Surveying the feast, he asked, "What are the rest of you going to eat?"

"Ha, ha," Elsa said, then stuck out her tongue at him.

Just as Cade began to wonder if Ethan would acknowledge Ally's presence, his brother turned to her and gave his million-dollar smile. "Ethan Sutter. You're here to save Cade's butt, huh?"

Allyson's brows arched. "I'm not sure about the butt-saving part, but I'm Ally Hamilton." She held out her hand.

Instead of shaking it, Ethan lifted her hand to his lips and kissed it. He shot a mocking glance at Cade from the corner of one cat-gold eye. Smug son of a bitch.

"Welcome to Hope Creek, Miss Hamilton," Ethan said. "I've been telling Cade we needed help."

Since when? Cade bit his tongue, aching to cuss his brother out but reluctant to start a feud with company at the table.

Allyson blushed as Ethan released her hand, then she reached for an ear of corn.

Cade curled a hand around his water glass and studiously avoided acknowledging Ethan's ridicule. "Allyson, will you need anything else to get settled in?"

She looked up at him and Cade felt a poke of satisfaction that he'd turned her attention away from his irritating brother. "I don't think so," she said. "Bailey's in the empty stall you gave me, and I've got the food I meant to leave him at the kennel. All I need is a tour of the pastures to get some soil samples."

"I'll do it," offered Ethan before anyone else could answer.

What the hell? This morning, Ethan had wanted nothing to do with the plant biologist. Now, he eyed her as if she were tonight's dessert. Kincade tried for his most indifferent expression. "You have to get the cows in."

Shrugging, Ethan piled salad and steak onto his plate. "The girls can handle them. They're all in the lower pasture."

"Don't volunteer me," Morgan cut in. "You still owe me for the hay baling last summer." She laid a slice of steak on Allyson's plate.

Ethan grabbed a roll and began buttering it. "I paid you back for that."

"Oh, no, you didn't," insisted Morgan.

"I will take care of the tour," Kincade broke in, telling himself he only offered so his siblings would stop bickering.

A devilish grin spread across Ethan's face. "Okay, then." He stuffed half the roll into his mouth.

Gripping his fork, Cade hoped like hell Ethan quit pushing buttons before he got hurt. Did he *like* being this annoying?

"Thanks, Cade," Ally said, and offered him a smile that chased away his inner growl. She accepted a roll from the basket Morgan handed her. "Doctor Coonan tells me you've owned the ranch for seven years. Family business?"

"Foster family business," Elsa answered. "We grew up together at a foster home nearby. Ethan used to pull my braids and Cade would rescue me."

"Ethan got into more trouble than the rest of us combined, if I remember right," added Morgan.

"Except, of course, when Cade decided to take us hiking," Ethan cut in.

Dread shivered up Cade's spine. He sensed,

more than saw, his sisters freezing in their seats. He shot his brother a warning look, but Ethan ignored it and went on running his mouth.

Picking an ear of corn off the platter, Ethan slathered butter on it. "We all packed up expecting to go into the woods, but Kincade, in his infinite wisdom, brought us to this abandoned—"

"Ethan," Morgan interrupted. "Maybe Allyson would like to tell us about her work at the college."

Ethan glanced up long enough to notice Morgan's quelling stare. With a tilt of his head, he bit into the ear of corn.

Relief ricocheted through Cade's nerves. He stole a guilty look at Ally, whose gaze shifted around the table as she wondered, no doubt, what *hadn't* been said. Scrambling to cover the uncomfortable silence, he asked, "Do you need a soil sample from each pasture?"

"Ideally, yes," she said at last, "but we could start with the ones closest to the house and finish up with the rest tomorrow. Who owned the place before you got here?"

"An older couple. Got too tired to maintain it, but they were careful farmers," said Cade. "I have some of their records if you need to look at them."

"Sure. That'd be helpful," she replied, but something in her tone suggested she still wanted to hear what Ethan had been about to divulge.

Right. Cade had no intention of telling her about the accident that had caused their special abilities. He certainly didn't plan to tell her the accident was his fault.

Hell, maybe losing his power was payback for that.

He sat back. "I'm not real hungry after all, Morgan. Can you stick this in the fridge for me?" When his sister nodded, he stood up and steeled himself against the curiosity radiating across the table from Allyson. "I'll be out in the horse barn when you're ready to start work on the samples."

He avoided looking back as he left.

Outside, he breathed easier. Ethan had come too close to letting out the truth of their powers. He'd been a loose cannon since childhood, even before the accident—always ready to provoke Kincade's temper. More than once, Cade wondered if his foster brother might be better off far away from Hope Creek.

And then there was the way Ethan had been looking at Allyson—*Miss Hamilton,* Cade corrected himself. He stalked across the driveway to the horse barn and threw open the loading door with more force than necessary.

How dare he hit on a woman who'd been called here in a professional capacity? His brother had no respect.

The mare in the closest stall whinnied and stuck her nose through the grain hole in her stall door. He went to her and rubbed her velvety muzzle. "Hungry, are you?" he murmured. He went to the nearby grain bins and proceeded to fill each horse's bucket.

A succession of yips drew his attention to the stall across from Diablo's. He peered through the grill of the door.

Bailey sat in the straw, tail thrashing. "Now, I know you don't think you're eating sweet feed," Cade said, waving the empty scoop in his hand.

The dog whined and jumped up, slapping his forepaws against the door. His cocoa-brown eyes pleaded in the way only a puppy's could.

"All right, all right, you little ankle biter." Cade rolled back the door and knelt down.

The puppy bolted out the door and into his lap, wriggling and slobbering and thoroughly ecstatic. He laughed and scratched behind the pup's ears, wishing he could feel such exuberance. "Yeah, you haven't got much to worry about, furball. No fizzling gift, no dying crops. All you need to know is where your next meal and next belly rub are coming from."

As if he understood, the pup flopped onto his back and waved all four paws in the air. Chuckling, Cade scratched the pup's belly.

"So where should we start with the samples?" Ally called.

Startled, Cade rose to his feet. Bailey spilled off his lap and proceeded to bounce around the breezeway like a fuzzy ping-pong ball. Ally stood in the open loading doorway with a smile. "I was just doing the evening feed," he said, chagrined. Had she overheard his one-sided lament?

He busied himself putting away the grain scoop and checking the tidiness of the already-neat grain bins. "We can start with the main horse pasture right after I let them in for the night."

"Can I help?" She scooped Bailey into her arms before the pup could make a break for the open doorway, then came forward to deposit him back into his stall and shut the door.

"You any good with catching horses?"

She nodded. "My dad was always bringing home injured animals, so we lived with a virtual menagerie when I was younger."

"All right. Just stay clear of Diablo." Cade grabbed a halter off a nearby stall door and handed it to her. Their fingers brushed. A staticky tingle fluttered up his arm and froze him in place.

It couldn't be.

As soon as she took the halter, he spun away and stared at his open hand.

No hint of his power, no tingling, nothing. Had he imagined it?

"Is something wrong?" she asked behind him.

He fisted his hand as if he could capture that

phantom sensation. Disappointment welled in his gut, but he forced it back. He had no time to feel sorry for himself, not with her standing there, sharp-eyed and distracting. "Nope. Let's get the horses in." He reached for another halter and looped it over his shoulder without a single look behind him. "Your halter's for Penny. Gray mare. She'll come when you call her."

For a moment, he thought she'd say something more, but she nodded and went outside.

Damn, damn, damn. He'd had his power—had it, just for a second, he could have sworn it. He risked another glance at his work-roughened hands.

Time was, he could almost have seen the luminescent glow underneath his skin when his gift was in full force. But now...now, not even a flicker appeared in his callused, creased palms, even while he willed it to come.

"Kincade?" Ally called. "Someone's here."

He left the barn to find a familiar brown truck rattling up the driveway. "Wonderful. Brady Hart, our neighbor. He's been wanting to buy the ranch."

When the truck came to a stop, Brady got out with something tucked under his arm. Smiling his usual toothy smile, he ambled his husky frame up the rest of the drive and tipped his wide-brimmed cowboy hat. That was Brady for you. All charm on the surface, but with a core like cold steel. "Murphy," he greeted. "Came to return your drill." He handed it over.

Cade took it, waiting for the pleasantries to end. No way had Brady driven all the way over from Fox Hollow to return a tool he'd borrowed a lifetime ago. Was the man running out of excuses?

"How's your old tractor holding up?" Brady asked. "Get her fixed?"

"Well enough," Cade said.

"You know," the man added with a casual shrug,

"I've been thinking of adding to that offer I made you last week."

Cade stiffened. "No, thanks." They'd been dancing the waltz of bid and refusal for several months. Brady's interest seemed to have increased with the absence of Cade's power. As unobtrusively as possible, Cade clenched his hand again.

His neighbor's broad grin reappeared. "Well, you be sure to let me know if you change your mind. I could use some of that far pasture. Bought another fifty head of cattle at auction yesterday."

"We're actually looking into some options for improving the land," Ally piped up.

Cade stared at her. She bit her lower lip and a faint, intriguing blush spread across her cheeks. Realizing he was still looking, he gave himself a mental kick. "Brady, this is Allyson Hamilton. Allyson, Brady Hart."

"Nice to meet you," she said.

The man gave her a warm smile, then turned to Cade with an air of shrewd appraisal. "Guess I'll have to wait on that offer, then, eh? Be seein' you." He touched his hat brim once more.

"Guess so. See you, Brady." Cade watched the man lumber back down to his truck.

Brady Hart could wait until hell froze over. Hope Creek would go up for sale over Cade's dead body.

****

Open mouth, insert foot, Ally thought, cheeks flaming again. At this rate, she'd lose her job before the assignment was over.

Cade rubbed a hand through his sable-black hair. "So what was that all about?"

She wrung the straps of the halter in her hands. "I'm sorry, I just..."

"Didn't like him."

"Well, no... I mean, I don't want to insult him—"

Cade grinned. The shallow dimple flashed in his cheek, sending a pleasant little thrill through her body. "Didn't take you long to get an off impression of him, did it?"

Half a day here and she was already making enemies of people? Julie would get her job for sure.

Seized by a burst of determination, she stopped fidgeting with the halter. "I'm going to solve your problem, Kincade. Give me a week, and I swear you'll be able to grow AstroTurf in your pasture, if you want to."

A low chuckle issued from his throat. She couldn't tell if he was laughing at her statement, or at the enormity of the task she'd just set herself. Oh, God, could she fix it that fast? She didn't even know what the problem *was* yet.

His vivid green gaze lingered on her face as if he could read her thoughts. She almost thought he could. She'd never seen such an intense look. "Shall we?" he asked, waving toward the pasture gate.

Shaking out of it, she helped him bring in the horses one by one. Most went without protest, no doubt knowing their evening feed waited in the barn. Diablo, however, remained in the pasture with his ears pinned back. Standing beside her with halter in hand, Kincade sighed and opened the pasture gate.

"He's not fond of people, is he?" she called.

"He's not fond of much," admitted Cade.

"What happened?"

"He was caught in the barn fire."

Somehow, that simple answer chilled her more than a dramatic statement might have done. For the first time, she noticed the scars marring the stallion's glossy hide. "How awful. I'm surprised he'll even go into a barn after that. I'm not sure I blame him."

Cade grunted, then proceeded to circle wide

around the stallion. Diablo, obviously familiar with this routine, raised his head and stamped a hind hoof as if daring the man to come closer. From the horse's far side, Ally heard the slap of the leather halter against Cade's thigh. The stallion snorted and held his ground. Another slap. "Move it, grouchy," Cade said.

The stallion shook his mane and paced toward the gate. Ally couldn't help smiling, though she cut it short when Diablo approached and bared his teeth at her. She lunged away from the fence. The stallion snorted and tossed his head.

Something in the horse's rolling eye tugged at her heartstrings. "Easy, boy," she murmured, wanting to lay soothing hands on that damaged, twitching hide. "What's got you so antsy? A little thing like me couldn't hurt a big fellow like you."

Diablo's ears swiveled back, forward, back again, as if he were sizing her up. They came forward at last. His nostrils flared and he lowered his head to take a cautious sniff at her, breath whuffing into the silence.

The leather halter slipped over his head and Cade appeared close to the stallion's side. Diablo balked and tried to rear, but the man's firm grip prevented escape. Cade buckled the halter. "That'll teach you to bite at someone."

Frowning, Ally opened the gate and let them through. "Do you think... Could he be rehabilitated?"

"He's about as docile as he's going to get. We've tried it all already," Cade called over his shoulder.

I haven't, she found herself thinking. She followed at a safe distance, watching the swing of the stallion's powerful hindquarters, and then the clockspring-taut gait of the man leading him. Some secret tension lingered in Cade's broad shoulders, something more than the need to be on guard with the wary horse. She wondered if Cade might be complicating matters by communicating that tension to the horse without knowing it.

Her gaze trailed downward over Cade's flannel shirt to where he'd tucked it loosely into well-worn jeans. The corner of one back pocket had frayed and—oh, my. What an amazing butt. A perfect specimen of male—

"Cade?" Elsa called from the house's front porch. "Maryanne's on the phone. She says it's important."

Ally's appreciation for Cade's finer points shattered and an unexplainable prickliness settled into its place. Who was Maryanne?

"She can wait," Cade answered with a satisfying tone of annoyance.

From the porch steps, Elsa shifted and held up the cordless phone, one hand over the mouthpiece. "She says her dad's real sick. He's at the hospital in Browning."

Kincade's head snapped up. He paused at the barn doorway to squint over Diablo's back at his foster sister. "Give me ten minutes."

Maryanne Sagerton, Ally found out a short while later, was Kincade's ex-girlfriend and daughter of the town's mayor. Elsa gave only the most basic of details, but Ally gathered the relationship hadn't ended on a good note. Though he no longer spoke to Maryanne, who'd always valued money more than character, Cade apparently still respected her father.

That Maryanne was a one-time socialite only added to Ally's curiosity. Cade didn't seem the sort of man who'd hobnob with the champagne-and-caviar set. But then, what did she really know about him?

Preoccupied, Cade returned Diablo to his stall, then left Ally at her bunk while he answered Maryanne's phone call. When he returned, he was shrugging into a lightweight barn coat. "I'm sorry," he said, "but we'll have to cut the research short, unless you want Ethan to take you around to the pastures. I need to go into town."

Stubbornness reared its head. "I can wait," she replied. Would she even get her chance to prove her skills to Kincade, and by extension, to her department superiors? Cade seemed to treat her arrival as a necessary evil, a task that must be addressed instead of an opportunity to solve his problem. As if he thought the damage was done and her presence wouldn't help matters.

Casting about the small bunkroom, she spied her canvas tote on the trunk. She pulled it toward her and began poking through the stack of notebooks inside, trying not to clutch the bag like a security blanket.

"Want to come?"

Surprise and pleasure washed away her doubts. Maybe she'd been too quick to judge him. "To town? Yes, I'd like that."

"Good. You can tell me a little more about what you do, and we'll work out a schedule for the next few days."

She pulled a pink notebook and a pen from the bag and reached for her windbreaker with the other hand. "Perfect. I could use some new audiocassette tapes for my handheld recorder. I didn't have a chance to get any on the way here."

"That's fine. There's a general store on Main Street. Let's go." He led the way to his truck. "Passenger door's busted, so you'll have to get in from the driver's side," he said, holding the door for her.

"All right." She got in and slid across the bench seat. He vaulted into the truck beside her. The engine roared to life, and they were on their way.

She stared out the passenger window at the vast fields sweeping by as they drove the thirty miles to Sagerton. She wanted to ask about Maryanne's father, but Cade seemed content to let the radio fill the silence. The fizzy broadcast alternated between old country songs and a farm report, unable to pick up a good signal on either. "I don't think I've ever seen so much empty space," she said at last.

His gaze flicked toward her before settling back on the road. "Thought you were a farm girl."

"I am. Or I was. Working at the college, I'm sort of stuck living nearby in the city, and your ranch is even more isolated than my father's place." She gestured out the window toward the distant sunset-painted mountains.

"Too isolated?" The hint of a smile played along his mouth.

"On the contrary. At least you can hear yourself think out here," she responded. "You don't have wailing sirens or neighbors banging on your door at all hours."

He snorted. "Not unless you count Brady. The man's been getting inventive with his reasons for dropping by. Slicker than a greased pig."

"Why don't you sell part of your land?" she suggested, thinking of the fire-damaged barn and poor-quality feed. "The money could help with improvements."

He shot her a cutting look, as chilly as frosted emeralds, and she knew she'd made a mistake. "Hope Creek is our home. I'm not about to butcher it for the auctioneers." His gaze turned to his hands, which tightened on the steering wheel until his knuckles turned white.

Studying his rigid posture, Ally shrugged deeper into her windbreaker. The words *I'm sorry* faltered on her lips until he added, "What will you do if the problem isn't in the soil?"

The question caught her unprepared. She struggled to turn her attention from his cool attitude to the condition of his pastureland. "Well," she began, "insect or microbe damage might be preventing your crops from thriving. I know the area's had decent growing seasons the past couple of years, so it can't be weather. You've already said you're against artificial fertilizers."

"And I still am."

She thrust her chin into the air. "I said I'd help you, Kincade, and I plan to use every last resource I have."

His grip on the wheel loosened. "I'm sure you will." They said nothing further for the rest of the ride.

The town of Sagerton, Montana stretched along a couple of wide, paved streets bordered by trees and broad sidewalks. Street lamps were just beginning to flicker on in the dusk.

Cade pointed her in the direction of the Sagerton Market, then told her he'd meet her there in twenty minutes. His earlier tension seemed to have multiplied, and she guessed it must have something to do with the mysterious Maryanne.

She opened the door to the general market and a bell tinkled overhead.

"Evening," greeted a frost-haired man at the front counter. He squinted at her through a pair of bifocals. "Help you with something?"

"Dog leashes and cassette tapes for a mini-recorder?" she asked, letting the door swing shut behind her.

"Aisle six for the leashes, and five for the tapes. Mind the mop bucket by the endcap, there," the man said, then turned back to a thick catalog on the counter.

Ally followed the man's directions, skirting the bucket he'd mentioned. She picked up a new leash to replace Bailey's broken one, and then went to aisle five. Part way down, she found a selection of overpriced electronic items. She sighed to herself and picked up a package of cassette tapes. Mom-and-pop businesses just couldn't compete with big chain stores anymore.

"Kincade Murphy's in town, did you see?" she heard a female voice say from the next aisle.

"I saw his truck," responded another woman.

Not wanting to eavesdrop, Ally walked back down the aisle toward the counter to cash out until she heard the first woman add, "If you ask me, Maryanne's much better off without him. I never liked the look of that man, and too many strange things go on at that ranch."

Ally froze at the end of the aisle, cheeks burning with embarrassment even as she found herself unable to resist such a mysterious comment. She laid a hand on the handle of the mop standing in the bucket. What sort of strange things happened at Hope Creek?

"Hmmph," came the other voice. "You just tell me if Kincade can compete with Maryanne's new beau, anyway."

"What? Who?" The first voice sharpened with excitement over the dangling tidbit of gossip.

The second woman gave a laugh. "Oh, he's the handsomest thing I've ever seen. He's from Helena, and I think he must have a lot of money. I saw Maryanne wearing a new pair of diamond earrings at the barbecue last Sunday."

"Well, good for her, I say," the first voice said. Then, sounding like she hoped to spring some juicy news herself, she added, "Did you know her father's in the hospital?"

Ally took another step, intending to leave the women to their chatter, and then caught the first woman's next remark. "—I'll bet dollars to donuts that Kincade had something to do with Jimmy landing in the hospital. I just don't trust that young man, Vi. Not since that mine explosion when he was a boy. Who knows if he and his brother and sisters were lighting off firecrackers in there?"

Ally's hand twitched and knocked the mop out of the bucket. It clattered into a shelf of beauty products, which cascaded onto the vinyl tile.

Two elderly women rushed to her aid. "Oh, dear," said the shorter one, and Ally recognized her voice as belonging to one of the gossips. "Are you all right?"

"Let me help you," said the other. She set her enormous purse on a shelf and picked up the fallen mop.

Mortified, Ally scraped up a handful of shampoo bottles. "Thanks. I'm fine."

The taller woman eyed her until she felt like a bug under glass. "I don't believe we've met. Are you new in town?"

"Er...yes," Ally confessed. "Allyson Hamilton." She shook their hands, noting their expectant stares, but didn't elaborate. She had no desire to add fuel to the fire regarding their gossip about Kincade—even if she was curious, herself.

"Bea Mortimer," the taller woman said, "and this is Viola St. Christie. We're on the Ladies Auxiliary and we run the local church group." Again she stared at Ally as if waiting for her to reciprocate with more information.

Ally pushed the shampoo bottles back onto their shelf. "Thank you for your help. I'm sure we'll see each other soon."

She heard the *click-click* of heeled shoes behind her and realized the women were following her to the counter, but didn't look back.

The market door opened with a jingle and Kincade entered the store. "Ready to go, Ally?"

Uh-oh. Behind Ally, one of the women cleared her throat with as much condescension as a person could pack into the sound.

Cade's gaze shifted to a spot over her shoulder. "Evening, Bea. Vi."

"Mister Murphy," came Bea's icy voice.

Ally felt the women's stares boring into her back, and knew they were wondering just what kind of connection the stranger in town had with a black sheep like Kincade. *Well, that ought to keep the gossip mill running,* she thought.

Chapter Three

"Of all the nosy old biddies in town, you would run across Bea Mortimer and Viola St. Christie," Cade said, taking Ally's shopping bag from her. Street lamps cast a mellow glow up and down the sidewalk as he put her purchases in the cab of the truck.

"I didn't plan it," she protested.

Cade tried to ignore Ally's shrewd gaze, but found it much more difficult than sidestepping the prying of the town gossips. God only knew what crazy crimes those women had pinned on him now. That in itself didn't bother him—he'd grown used to the talk in the twenty-three years since the accident—but Ally's silent curiosity made his skin itch. He shooed her into the truck cab, then climbed in beside her.

She hadn't quite shifted to the passenger side before he got in, and their thighs brushed together. A lightning bolt of sensation tore through his body and his skin went from itchy to tingly. At once startled and hopeful, he searched his hands for evidence of his earth-healing power...but his palms showed no remnants of the force that had once flowed within.

Twice! Twice now, he'd felt that power surge.

Because of her.

What was it about this woman that brought snatches of the old sensation back? Furtively he studied her profile, not knowing what he was looking for. Some clue, perhaps, that she might have powers like he and his siblings had, which could have caused his body to react on a subconscious level. Something special that resurrected his sleeping—or absent—gift.

She had skin like porcelain and features just as delicate. High cheekbones, and a fine nose that kept from seeming too cold by the dusting of tiny freckles across its bridge. Beautiful eyes, large and long-lashed and made to drown a man. He stared a lot longer than necessary, fascinated with the wisp of flame-colored hair that had settled against her pale cheek.

She seemed not to notice his scrutiny. In fact, she was gazing out the passenger window at a man across the street. "Isn't that Brady Hart over there? Who's he with?"

Cade tore his gaze away to find Brady talking with a tall, polished man in khakis and a blazer. The two made an absurd contrast—Brady in his patched trousers and faded barn coat, and the stranger looking like he'd stepped off the glossy pages of a fashion magazine. "Don't know," Cade muttered, more to himself than to Ally. Brady made a short, choppy gesture, then took off his hat to rub a hand through his graying hair. Whoever the newcomer was, the two seemed to be having a heated discussion.

Ally turned away from the scene outside to Cade. "Is your friend's father all right?"

He raised an eyebrow. "Half an hour in town, and you're already sucked into the rumor mills?"

"But Elsa said he was really sick." Her cheeks colored a little.

"Jim's got an ulcer, but the doctors are managing it. Maryanne overreacts." He started the truck's engine and pulled away from the curb, not wanting to dwell on his ex, but the thought of her stuck like a porcupine quill under his skin.

She'd begged and pleaded and finally cajoled

him into a cup of coffee at the Main Street Diner. They began by talking about Jim's ulcer. Somehow, she steered the discussion onto their past relationship. Cade cut the talk short and walked out on her. He couldn't have said if she were trying to dredge up old anger or to apologize, but he doubted she'd had the latter in mind. Regret had never been Maryanne's strong suit.

Women. Trouble with a capital No Way.

Ally pulled her shopping bag across the truck seat and stuffed her notebook into it. "I didn't mean to sound nosy."

"Never mind," he said, turning his attention to the road home. "What are your plans for the ranch?"

She brightened. "After I collect soil samples, I send them to the lab for testing. If I find something as simple as a nutrient deficiency, most farms fix it by adding a water-soluble form of that nutrient when they irrigate their crops. Fertilizer's not the only solution," she hurried to add. "I'm actually working on an organic farming project at the college. Some of the ideas might work for you. Crop rotation, letting a field lie fallow for a season... But I'm sure you do all that. There are more possibilities."

Cade gave a noncommittal grunt and forced himself not to fidget. He knew full well that the problem began and ended with him, but he couldn't help hoping she'd somehow find enough of an improvement for his land to hold him over until his power came back.

You're fooling yourself, said a mocking voice in his head, sounding a lot like Ethan. *You can't expect her to be your crutch when the problem isn't even external.* What with one thing and another, he felt like he'd been putting Allyson's efforts off all day.

Maybe he had. If she stayed the full week and still couldn't find him a solution, he'd have to admit Hope Creek was doomed.

He pressed on the accelerator and the engine revved in protest. "Why don't we go home and get a couple of those samples?"

"In the dark?" she asked.

"It shouldn't take much to get a couple samples of dirt, should it?" He avoided her gaze, focusing on the road as they left Sagerton. The silence for the first few miles deafened him and he almost wished for the static of the radio again.

"Mister Murphy," she said at last, "why don't you tell me why I'm really here?"

The question sent a cold chill through him. He wondered for one wild minute whether she saw right through his charade. "For exactly the reason I wrote the letter to your department," he answered with feigned calm.

Her stare settled on him like a yoke. "Either you want me to help you with my hands tied behind my back, or you don't think anything I find is going to solve your problem."

Yep. She saw right through him, all right. Her frank appraisal stirred up the guilt buried inside him. Would he never be free of the lies surrounding his life? And even if he could escape the lies, would he endanger his family doing so? "What do you need from me to make your work easier?" he asked, forcing the words out.

"Well, the soil samples are a start. But you'll need to be open to suggestions," she said. "If it comes down to fertilizing, wouldn't you rather do that and keep your ranch running than lose it?"

And there was the rub. He had no idea how fertilizing his land might affect his ability to grow anything using his power alone—assuming his power ever returned. Either he'd have to risk the fertilizer, or risk losing his family's home.

When they returned to the ranch, Elsa, Morgan, and Ethan were in the yard under the glow of the house's floodlight. Allyson's dog danced around Elsa's feet. As soon as Cade and Ally emerged from the truck, Ethan stalked toward them with an uncharacteristic frown of sobriety on his face. Without waiting for a greeting, he thrust a paper into Cade's hand.

Cade turned his attention to the crumpled white sheet. The single, computer-printed line on the page sent a wave of ice water rushing through his veins.

I know all about you, Kincade Murphy. Leave town while you have the chance.

Struggling to avoid showing his alarm, he raised his gaze to Ethan's. His brother stared back with the same effort of calm on his face. Ethan's shoulder twitched once, the motion almost imperceptible in the dim yard. No, then—he didn't know who had sent the letter.

Cade turned a glance toward Allyson. She looked back and forth between Ethan and him, clearly interpreting their agitation. Cade thrust words out. "Let's start on those soil samples." He shoved the note in his back pocket and pivoted toward the barn.

Ally jogged after him. "If there's a problem—"

"Nope," he answered. He sent a cutting stare toward his siblings and hoped they understood he'd take care of their unknown threat.

As soon as his blood thawed.

****

What was the matter with Kincade now? Ally blew a frustrated sigh that fluttered her bangs. They'd gathered five soil samples—one from each of the nearest pastures—and all the while he'd been silent as a cemetery. Tension radiated from him in sharp, unsettling bursts, distracting her while she capped the glass containers and made notes in her book. She wanted to ask him if he needed to talk, but one look at the storm brewing in his dark green eyes had trapped the question behind her teeth.

He'd sent her off to bed with the barest of civility, and it stung her pride after all her earnest efforts to help him that evening. She tossed and turned and buried her head under the pillows, blotting out the weak moonlight peeking through the curtained window, but sleep eluded her.

A muffled thump and whinny issued from the barn outside her door. Deciding it was as good an excuse as any, she got up to check on the horses. She pulled on her thick terry bathrobe and sneakers, then opened the bunkroom door with a creak.

The sound had come from Diablo, stabled at the end of the barn and separated from the other horses by an empty stall. The stallion paced in tight circles, tossing his head. The straw-muffled ring of his shod hoofs filled the barn. He struck the stall door and it shuddered. "Easy, big guy, easy. There's no reason to make a fuss. Nothing in this barn is going to hurt you."

"Can't say the same for you," hissed a voice.

Yelping, Allyson spun around. A figure dressed in black, his face hidden by a ski mask, stood in her path with a huge, gleaming knife. In the stall across the breezeway, Bailey whined.

The intruder's gloved hand shot out and he snatched the front of her bathrobe. He shoved her backward. Ally pitched against Diablo's stall. A scream bubbled up, but the intruder clapped his hand over her mouth before it could escape. "Wouldn't do that," he said, and she felt the cold edge of the knife blade as it pressed against her throat.

She stilled at once. Behind her, Diablo snorted and the muffled clang of his hoofbeats increased. "What do you want?" she choked out when the man lowered his hand.

"You to leave. Now." His hot breath puffed

across her face.

The stall door's grill jabbed into the back of her head until tears pricked at her eyes. She whimpered, and Bailey yipped uncertainly from the opposite stall. "Why?" she asked, trembling. "I'm just a scientist. I—"

"*Shut up,*" he snarled. "Just get your stuff and go." He knocked her head against the grill with his forearm.

Stars burst behind her eyes. Diablo gave a shrill whinny, and then another. Bailey started barking, throaty puppy *aroo-o-os* that echoed down the breezeway.

The intruder stepped back and Ally tried to bolt. He backhanded her across the face and her vision exploded into whiteness. She spun and fell, blinded by pain, and slammed to the ground with a cry. Pounding footsteps rang in her ears. She heard the creak of the door, and then only Bailey's whining and Diablo's angry kicks against the stall. Consciousness wavered. She struggled to keep it, but her senses started slipping away.

"Allyson? Allyson!"

Footsteps again, and then strong arms, lifting her back onto her feet. She groaned and touched a hand to her aching head, and then the white blur faded and she could see again.

Kincade's jewel-green eyes bored into hers, bright with concern. "What happened?"

"Burglar," she gasped out, waving an arm toward the swinging door at the end of the barn.

Cade didn't even look away. "You okay?"

She nodded. He let go and strode stiff-bodied toward the other door to look out into the night. "I'll be right back in. Yell if you see anything." He slipped outside.

The door on the opposite end of the barn hung open where Cade had entered. Still dizzy, Ally stumbled toward it and stood trembling in the doorway. She squinted into the darkness, half expecting the intruder to return.

Back on the barn's other end, Bailey started howling. Allyson shut the door, then went to his stall to get him. He leaped into her arms, licking her face and whining. "Shh," she urged, holding him close until he quieted again. She kept him in her arms while she waited for Kincade, as if the pup could shield her from further attack, and paced the breezeway. She ran shaking fingers through his soft fur while her head ached and her cheek throbbed.

On her fourth walk up the breezeway, the other door creaked behind her. She whirled to face it.

Cade stepped back inside. "Whoever it was, he's long gone."

Drawing a breath that couldn't quite fill her lungs, Ally put Bailey back in his stall.

Cade approached her. His brows drew together and he brushed a hand against her aching cheek, smoothing back her hair. Ally felt the tension in his fingers in spite of his gentle touch. "Are you okay?" he asked again.

"No." She groaned, wondering wildly if her cheekbone was broken. "He hit me."

Cade's arm slid around her shoulders. He murmured to the restless stallion, then helped Allyson back to the bunkroom.

While he put together an ice pack, she sank onto the bed and wondered aloud, "How did you get here so fast from the house?"

"I was out walking. Couldn't sleep." His boots thumped on the plank floor as he returned to the bed, and then he crouched beside it. He held the ice pack to her aching cheek. Slowly, the chill began to numb her pain. "Did you get a good look at the guy?" he asked.

"Yes. No." Tears welled up, blurring his face. "I

mean, I was so scared, I—I didn't see anything clearly. I don't remember..."

"All right. Just take it easy." He sat beside her. "Did he say anything to you?"

Shuddering, she answered, "He wants me to leave."

"Leave Hope Creek?" Cade's voice rose as he spoke.

She glanced at him, only to find that his expression had gone carefully blank. "I guess—I don't know," she stammered. "I didn't exactly have time to get clarification."

Muscles worked in his jaw. "I'm sorry," he said. "Why don't you come up to the house for the rest of the night? The couch isn't that uncomfortable."

You're uncomfortable, though. She watched him grind his teeth and wondered why her nearness bothered him so.

As much as she disliked encroaching on his privacy, she liked the idea of another visit from the intruder even less. "Let me get my clothes for tomorrow."

Cade waited while she gathered her things. "Your late-night caller broke the lock on the door out there. I'll get a new one on it in the morning. The loading doors latch from the inside, so he wouldn't be able to get in again unless he tried from the hayloft hatch. No one's that stupid—it's too far up from ground level." He took her bag once she'd filled it with clothes and toiletries. "Meantime, I'll send Ethan out here to look after the barn tonight."

"I wouldn't want to drag him out of his bed," Ally protested.

A wry smile curled Cade's lips. "He needs the discipline."

His smile helped warm away her chills, just as his voice calmed her jitters. The knots in her muscles loosened as he walked her up to the house.

He woke Ethan, who, for once, had no snappy remarks. The redheaded man shrugged on his coat and left the house as silent as a ghost.

Cade insisted Ally sit on the generous plaid couch in the greatroom, where she could see across a counter into the kitchen while he made cocoa. "I don't want to keep you up any longer than I have," she said. "I'm all right, really."

"I want some cocoa, that's all," he responded. "Did I mention I'm a chocoholic? I need a nightly fix of the stuff, or I lose it."

Moonlight streamed in from the bank of windows along the greatroom's back wall and cast the shadows of the rough-hewn roof beams onto the vaulted knotty pine ceiling. She toed off her sneakers and dug her toes into the plushy area rug in front of the couch.

He came back with two steaming cups and set them down on the large antique sled that doubled as a coffee table. He crossed the greatroom, then stoked a fire in the river-rock fireplace on the room's other side. "It gets a little cold in here at night," he said when he returned and sat down. He pulled a wool blanket from the back of the couch and laid it in her lap. "Need pillows?"

She shook her head, glancing at the mound of plump pillows on the couch. "Not if you don't mind me using these." She ran a hand along one to test its softness and her fingers sank into it. Perfect. She saw why Cade wanted so much to hold onto this place. It sank into the soul.

He shook his head and raised his mug, but didn't drink. A frown tugged at his mouth. "I'm sorry about the burglar."

"Why should you apologize? You didn't ask him to break into the barn, did you?" she asked, attempting humor that she didn't feel.

"I'm just glad you weren't hurt."

She nodded, but she had to admit that his company chased away the rest of her shivers.

Boy, did it. Firelight flickered across his face as he stared at her. Ally's heartbeat thumped faster. Jitters bloomed in her belly. She watched the flame's glow play across the curve of his mouth, and before she realized what she was doing, she licked her own lips.

Good Lord, Allyson, she scolded herself. She ought to have been ashamed, staring at him like some wanton floozy. He'd invited her in only to protect her from being attacked on his property, after all.

He studied her with disturbing intensity, as if she were the only thing in this beautiful room worth looking at. "Something wrong?"

"Just, er, wishing for my notebook."

"In the middle of the night?"

"Well...that's when I do most of my best work. I start writing, and sometimes it jogs an idea that's been hiding all day." Her face flamed with more than the pain of her bruised cheek.

His lips curved into a grin and her pulse skipped. The moonlight spilling into the greatroom silvered his hair. Coupled with the glow from the fire, it turned him into some otherworldly creature from the myths of long ago. Ally smiled at her flight of fancy, until she caught a faint whiff of evergreens. *Probably potpourri,* she thought with an inward chuckle. *Or an open window.* She buried her nose in her cup and took a long drink of warm, creamy cocoa.

He waved a finger at his mouth. "You, uh... Whipped cream moustache."

"Oh." She giggled and skimmed her lip with the tip of her tongue. The sugary whipped cream melted into her mouth. "Gone?" she asked.

Cade's grin vanished. He watched her with

those unreadable jewel eyes for a moment. "Nope," he said, his voice low and husky. He raised his thumb to brush the corner of her lips.

The moment his fingers touched her skin she froze. A tidal wave of desire swamped her and left her torn with indecision. *Kiss him,* taunted a voice in the back of her mind. *How many men ever look at you like that?*

No, no, no, no, no, she chanted back, as if the mantra alone could keep her from making a fool of herself. *Do you* want *to lose this job?*

Cade's hand slipped to her cheek, where the heat of his palm soothed her aching bruise. "You should get someone to look at that," he said.

"It's all right. I'll be fine," she said. Her breath seemed to have deserted her.

He turned her cheek gently to examine it. His gaze shifted back to hers, glowing in the firelight. He lowered his hand again.

Ally felt his thumb skim her knuckles, but his stare held hers like it was riveted there.

Her heartbeat pounded into her throat.

The rough pads of his fingers curled around hers and brushed her hypersensitive palm. The touch shot up her arm, down her spine, and sank into her most secret places with a heat that rattled her every nerve.

Only when he dropped his gaze to her hand could she gain a breath.

He stared at her fingers for a moment. Faint lines appeared between his brows, as if studying her hand could provide some cosmic answer. "Good night, Miss Hamilton," he said at last. He lifted her hand and kissed the back of it, more rough than sweet. "Get some rest."

He rose from the couch and left the room. Ally shrugged into the wool blanket, chilled now that he wasn't there to warm her through with a simple look. She studied her hand, wondering what had so fascinated him about it.

Her stare wandered to the coffee table.

Kincade hadn't touched his cocoa at all.

Chapter Four

Kincade beat the sunrise out of bed by several hours, and gathered the parts to replace the broken barn door's lock while Ally was still asleep. He needed no flashlight to find his way to the horse barn. For seven years, he'd walked the exact same morning route on his ranch.

Hopefully, he'd get his power back in time, so that his morning routine could get nice and stale over another seven years.

The early-morning chill seeped through the open collar of his barn coat as he flipped on the lights. Ethan had taken care of the morning rounds; the horses were already out to pasture. Down the aisle, Bailey gave a few sleepy-sounding yips and fell silent once more.

The molasses scent of sweet feed lingered in the air. *Scatterbrain,* Cade scolded silently, shutting the grain bin Ethan had left open.

Then again, there was that saying about glass houses and stones. Since he'd been up, Cade's own thoughts kept drifting back to last night. Over and over, he relived that alarming moment when he'd almost let his lips fall on Allyson's, instead of brushing her knuckles and then fleeing the room. He had trouble enough without succumbing to some inane teenage urge to maul the woman who'd come to his ranch to help him. And she had enough problems finding him a solution, without his adding further to the mess.

Irritated, he set his tools down by the broken door and began work. He pulled the old handle off and plugged the new one into its place, then fished a screw out of the lockset package and shoved it into the hole on the handle plate. When he jabbed at it with the screwdriver, the tool slipped and stabbed his other hand.

Pain flared along his nerves. He swore and shook his wounded hand, berating himself. She'd been here a day, and already he couldn't concentrate on something as stupid as a minor repair. God help him if he had to work with Diablo today. He'd be as good as trampled.

Hmm. Ethan would have to deal with the stallion. Cade needed his focus to deal, for starters, with that so-called burglar. The man had to be connected somehow with the note Kincade received earlier that day. Break-ins didn't just happen out of the blue on a ranch set a good mile back from the road.

"Cows are out," Ethan said behind him.

Cade looked back over his shoulder. Ethan paused to open the door of the bunkroom and stare inside. "Looking for something in there?" Cade asked, letting a touch of frost into his voice.

Ethan flicked the brim of his cowboy hat so it sat farther back on his head. "Nope. Is Miss Fix-It still in the house?"

"If she isn't in the bunkroom, she would be, wouldn't she? It's four in the morning," Cade said. He dusted his hands off on his jeans, then gathered up the clutter from his work.

Shrugging, Ethan snagged a lead line off one of the stall doors and began making knots in it. "Just making sure she's sleeping well," he said.

"I'm sure she's delighted with the couch. Where did you sleep?" Cade asked as an unpleasant image of Ethan lying comfortably in Allyson's bed snapped into his mind.

"I slept in the stall with that yappy puppy,"

Ethan shot back. He took off his cowboy hat and turned it around to reveal a mangled section on the brim. "She owes me a hat. He chewed it."

"That hat's practically as old as I am," said Cade, "and you never cared about it before."

Ethan untied the lead line and started another knot. "Any idea who sent you that note?"

Ah, there was the real reason for Ethan's chit-chat. His brother never came right to the point of a serious issue, preferring to dodge it as if he were dancing with a speeding train. Cade dumped the broken lock in a trashcan. "Could be anybody, for all I know. We aren't exactly beloved pillars of the community." He started toward the tackroom.

"What about Maryanne?" Ethan suggested, following him.

They entered the tackroom and Cade inhaled the pleasantly pungent odors of tanned leather and saddle soap. Snatching a bridle and looping it over his shoulder, he said, "If she knows what's good for her, Maryanne wouldn't threaten me. I've got dirt on her that would make what's left of her daddy's hair curl."

Ethan perked up. "What kind of dirt?"

"The kind you aren't going to hear about," Cade said, and pushed his foster brother toward the saddle racks. "Get the black saddle and tack up Dancer. You're getting fence duty."

"Fence duty? Why do I get the fun jobs?" Ethan complained. He hated having to make the entire circuit of Hope Creek to inspect and repair fences. The job required someone willing to spend lots of time out in the pastures with nothing but wind and songbirds for company. Exactly why Cade loved it.

Grumbling, Ethan hoisted up the saddle and Dancer's bridle, then stalked out the door. "By the way, you get to exercise Diablo this afternoon, too," Cade called.

47

"You suck," Ethan's voice floated back to him.

Cade allowed himself a brief smile and returned to work.

He crossed the pitted gravel driveway to the cow barn, then finished mucking the stalls Ethan hadn't yet done. After that, he went to the hay shed for fresh straw. By then the sun had begun to rise, and sleepy birds were beginning their morning songs.

He'd just trucked several bales of straw back in the farm's small utility wagon when Allyson arrived in the cow barn, freshly scrubbed and toting an enormous Thermos. "Coffee. Thought you could use it," she said. "Elsa and Morgan say you've been up since three."

Cade hefted a bale of straw out of the wagon bed, then dropped it into one of the stalls and cut the twine binding it. He examined her, trying not to be obvious, and saw a faint bruise on her cheek. "Sleep okay?"

"Better than I thought I would," she admitted. "I had breakfast, too. Yours is waiting for you up at the house."

"I'll get it later." He took a pitchfork and spread straw out in the nearest stalls.

"I'm sorry I wasn't up earlier to help you with chores," she said.

"You're not here to do chores—but thanks."

She poured out a generous cup of coffee and handed it to him. "I should be thanking you."

He wrapped a leather-gloved hand around the Thermos cup and tipped it to his lips. The hot beverage slid down his throat and he swallowed, letting it warm his belly. "Why should you thank me?"

"You were very kind to me last night. You didn't need to stay up to make sure I was all right."

"You were assaulted on my property," he said, wrestling with discomfort at the gratitude in her eyes. Whenever she looked at him, it seemed she could see right down through the cracks in his soul to the man he hid from everyone else, even his family. He wanted to push something between them. A straw bale. The tractor. The whole barn.

She fixed him with a pointed, dove-gray stare. "Thank you just the same. Accept a compliment, will you?" She turned her attention to the remaining bales of straw in the wagon trailer. "Can I at least help you with this before starting on the rest of the soil samples?"

"If you want. You can leave a bale in the wagon bed and cut the twine there. It'll be easier to pull straw from there than carry a whole bale yourself. They're kind of heavy."

She found another pair of leather gloves, then, smiling at him, lifted one of the fifty-pound bales out of the wagon bed. She beamed and carried the bale away to the stalls farther down.

Impressed, he watched her go. Not afraid of a little hard work, that one. Maryanne would never have dreamed of risking her manicure to help him muck a stall.

They finished the cow barn together and Cade shared the rest of the coffee with Ally. They stopped at the horse barn to get tack, and then went to the paddocks to collect a pair of horses. "The remaining pastures are too far away to walk," he explained. "I'll tack up the horses if you want to gather your equipment. Got anything that won't fit in a saddlebag?"

"I don't think so," she said.

While she went to the bunkroom to get her supplies, he selected the horses. He chose Smoky, a steady steel-gray gelding, and Rumble Seat, a flashy chestnut son of Diablo. The youngster still had a thing or two to learn about being a ranch horse. Cade hoped the gelding might teach the colt how to behave if he kept the two together often enough.

Ally returned with an armload of technical-looking equipment. "I meant to ask you if we could go up into the mountains too. I'd like to see what kind of plant life is hiding up there. As a comparison, sort of."

"I don't see why not," he said, then helped her stow her gear in Smoky's saddlebags. As he packed a set of small glass vials, her slender arm brushed his. He stiffened and stole a look at her. She frowned at something in her obnoxious bright pink notebook and nibbled at her lower lip. Cade's attention fixed on her mouth and stayed there. All sorts of unbidden images paraded through his head.

A snort yanked his attention into the paddock beside the barn. Diablo stood several yards from the fence with pinned-back ears, pawing the ground and shaking his mane. Relieved to have a distraction, Kincade laced his fingers together. "Rider up."

"Thanks." Her long red hair swung forward as she leaned close and stepped into his cupped hands. Her palm settled on his shoulder.

Her touch shot through his body like an electric shock, even through the layers of barn coat and flannel shirt. Cade sucked in a breath and held it, willing himself not to breathe in the scent of her hair. She smelled like Morgan's decadent strawberry pie—sweet, inviting, beyond forbidden. But dessert had never looked this good. His nerves sizzled.

Get a grip, Murphy. The quicker you get her on the horse, the quicker you can get away from her. He gave himself a mental shake as she settled into the saddle and he focused on shortening the stirrups for her.

When he finished with the gelding, he adjusted Rumble's tack. He heard Ally cluck her tongue and looked over the colt's back.

She had drawn her mount alongside the

paddock fence to stare at the stallion.

Diablo snorted again and bolted toward the fence. "Allyson—" he warned.

Her horse shied, but she held him firm until he settled. Diablo skidded to a stop just before the fence, digging at the turf with one shod forehoof. Allyson lowered her head, appearing engrossed in Smoky's mane, but Cade saw her watching the stallion from the corner of her eye. "Whoa, there, handsome fella."

Diablo shook his head. His tail lashed once, twice. She kept talking, a musical, indiscernible rise and fall of words. Diablo's skin shivered. Cade thought his might, too, under that verbal caress. Finally the stallion's ears pricked forward. He lowered his head and his muscles stopped twitching. Ally grinned and turned her horse away from the fence.

Cade's mouth opened, but he had no idea what he'd been about to say. She'd calmed that devil horse with mere words—but what if he'd charged forward and jumped the fence instead of subsiding? He could have kicked Smoky and sent her flying. She might have broken bones—or her neck. He marshaled his face into a stern scowl. "I said stay clear of him."

Allyson caught his eye and her triumphant smile faded. "I'm sorry," she said. She glanced over her shoulder at the stallion, who had begun cropping grass at the edge of the fence. "But he's such a beautiful horse. There isn't any harm in me talking to him, is there?"

Kincade swung up into his saddle, then took the reins in one hand. "For the record," he added, "that's about as nice as he's been to anybody in months." A tiny spot of warmth settled in his chest, a grudging admiration for her skill at soothing Diablo when he'd failed at it so many times. The stallion must have sensed something different about her.

Trotting his horse ahead of hers, Cade led the way toward the back pastures. He glanced at his gloved hand, fisted around the reins, and remembered the tingling sensations of her touch. He ached to touch her again, skin to skin, and see if his lost power might resurface.

Something *was* different about Allyson Hamilton. And if he didn't watch it, she'd discover that something was vastly, freakishly different about Kincade and his foster family, too.

****

The sprawling field in the far pasture stole Ally's breath. Long grass swayed in the crisp breeze. A large pond glittered in the late-morning sun. Beyond it rose the mountains, cloaked in pines. She opened her mouth to speak but shut it again, awed in spite of having lived in Montana all her life. The gorgeous vista more than made up for the ranch's run-down first impression. How could Cade *not* want to preserve a home like this?

"Our land goes all the way back into the mountains," he called back to her. "We get a lot of deer and elk first thing in the morning, so you might see tracks here and there once we move up outside the fence."

"It's lovely," she said at last. She scanned the grasses and wildflowers as they passed the pond, then looked up the mountain slopes at a creek running down toward his property. Around the water line of the creek and pond, the vegetation grew sparse and weedy. "Can we stop for a moment?" she asked.

He circled back and drew alongside. "What caught your eye?"

"Just taking a look," she murmured, slipping down from the saddle. She bent and pulled up a handful of grass from the water's edge. The blades had faded, though they should have been full and verdant green this time of year. She put a few samples of the soil and vegetation in her saddlebags, and then, as an afterthought, capped a sample of the water as well.

He remained silent while she worked, waiting aboard Rumble Seat and holding her horse's reins. She felt his eyes on her and a shiver sped up her back as though he'd brushed his warm, callused fingers along her spine. Her skin tingled with the memory of his hand holding hers last night. Unsettled, she hurried back to her horse. When he offered to help her up, she shook her head and swung into the saddle on her own.

They rode to the end of the pasture and out the back gate. As they ascended into the foothills, the hairs on the back of Ally's neck prickled. Turning in her saddle, she searched for movement in the trees, but saw nothing unusual. She stared back over her shoulder down the slope to the ranch. The pasture below was wide and bare of cover, all the way back to the barns.

Her horse's hooves slipped on loose stones. She turned back to the front, giving Smoky his head so he could regain his balance, and directed her gaze between the horse's ears where it should have been. It locked on Cade's broad back, impressive even under the roomy barn coat.

He sat a horse like he was born to it. She stared at the way his muscular legs gripped the horse's barrel. His body swayed with the animal's motion as though they were one creature, like the powerful centaurs of Greek myth. Her fanciful thoughts began to run away with her, and she imagined Kincade dressed in armor, his handsome face stern with the shadows of an oncoming epic battle. She laughed at her own silliness.

He paused his horse in a clearing where the trees widened out. One corner of his mouth quirked upward until that mesmerizing dimple appeared. "Care to share?"

"Ah, nothing." She grinned back, relishing the fresh air and the warm sun on her shoulders as they rode higher into the trees. The creek flowing down the mountainside burbled away somewhere to her left. This sure beat being stuck at a counter indoors, surrounded by test tubes, computers, and microscopes. If she succeeded at this field assignment more might follow, and that might lead the way to a research grant. That would trump Julie and her mile-long legs for sure. No way could Doctor Coonan pass her by with dollar signs in his eyes.

Cade still watched her, and she realized she'd been staring at him for several moments. Embarrassed, she walked Smoky forward again. "How'd you get to be a horseman?"

"Just got lucky, I guess." He paused for her to draw alongside. "I took a job on this ranch a while back, and when it came up for sale, that was it."

Studying him as they turned onto a dirt trail, Ally imagined what life must have been like for him growing up. *He was old when he was young,* Morgan had told her. *Cade's the glue that kept us together.*

What must it be like to be the man who kept this makeshift family from falling apart? Had those broad shoulders borne that weight since he was a child?

"Look," he said, pointing.

She peered in the direction of his extended arm, through a stand of trees into another clearing. Frozen between a pair of slender pines and shadowed in morning mist was a pair of mule deer. "They're beautiful," she whispered. As if her words had freed them, the pair bounded away into the forest.

Turning to Kincade, she found him watching her. A snap of awareness sped through her body.

"What?"

He swept a hand at the barren ground of the trail. "This look like a good enough spot to stop for more soil samples?"

"Sure," she answered, dragging her gaze away from him with a pang of regret.

They slipped from their horses together. Cade led his mount to the edge of the worn dirt trail and tied its reins to a sturdy branch. He turned back to take her horse's reins as she led the animal closer. The motion brought him up short just inches away.

His body went rigid as stone. Time stopped and held its breath with her.

The warmth in her face could have been the sun. The tingle on her skin might have been the light breeze lifting her hair. But only the green, green depths of his eyes caused such a quivering in her belly. Standing mere inches away, he studied her like some ancient mystery.

Morgan was more right than she knew. If Ally had to go by Cade's eyes alone, she couldn't have said how old he was—but it might have been centuries.

He loomed close enough for his body heat to draw a sharp contrast to the cool mountain air. His gaze dropped to her mouth. She heard the soft hiss of his indrawn breath, and he took half a step closer. Her heartbeat doubled speed. "We shouldn't do this," he murmured.

For once in her life, she didn't care what she should or shouldn't do. Everything ceased to exist but the phantom heat emanating from him. Something in her whispered that she'd never get this chance again. She took a breath to slow her pounding heart and closed the distance between their bodies. "What if I want to?"

A haunted look flashed across his face. Faint lines formed between his brows. "*I* shouldn't, Ally."

Disappointment speared her. Unwilling to let him see how much his refusal hurt, she turned away.

His warm, rough hand slipped into hers. Surprised, she turned back.

He stepped closer and rooted her to the spot with a heated stare. "I didn't say I didn't want to." His breath fanned her face. He seemed to come to a decision, and then his lips touched hers.

The feather-light kiss sent a heady burst of longing spinning through her body. Oh, sweet heaven. She closed her eyes and leaned into the warm, solid length of him, wanting more, but his mouth remained soft as spring grass. She gave herself up to his unhurried exploration.

The scent of him mingled with the smells of pine and sun-warmed earth. He made a low sound that shot straight to her core, then clutched folds of her lightweight jacket to pull her closer. Ally moaned and parted her lips as his tongue sought entrance to her mouth. Holy Toledo, she was kissing her client. She'd get fired for sure. *But oh, don't stop,* she pleaded silently. The buzz of morning insects filled her ears.

No. Not insects—much louder. What the heck was that?

He broke away then and raised a hand to rake it through his dark brown hair. "Bad idea. I'm sorry, Allyson." He took her horse and retreated, tying the animal up with quick, efficient movements.

Confused, she followed. "I don't want you to be sorry." She laid a hand on his shoulder and pulled him back to face her.

He stared at his hands with such intensity that a chill skated up the back of her neck. She strode forward, looking for blood. "Cade?"

He turned his stare on her for a breathtaking moment, and then it shifted to the ground. He knelt and laid a hand on the barren earth of the trail.

"What are you doing?" she asked, scanning the ground around them.

"Looking for...something," he said, almost too quiet to be heard. She caught a glimpse of something aching and vulnerable in his expression before his guard slammed in place again. Once again, he was the stoic rancher who kept his thoughts well hidden. He reminded her of an empty meadow, silent at first look, but teeming with life and activity once you got close enough to discover it. Robbed of that sunshine-warm gaze and the heat of his embrace, she shrugged deeper into her jacket.

Cade stood and went back to the horses. He untied Smoky and brought him to her side. "Let's ride."

His husky voice stirred that longing in her again, and she thought about giving in to it and touching him. *Don't be a fool,* she scolded herself. *He doesn't want you. He's made that clear.* She grabbed the reins and a handful of mane, and climbed aboard Smoky by herself.

They took a few more samples from random places in the woods. Ally surveyed the collection of jars in her saddlebag, proud of her morning's work. By the time they'd finished and started back down the slopes toward the ranch, the day had warmed enough to make her jacket unnecessary. Riding ahead of Cade, she paused her horse to shrug the extra layer off. "Once I get these samples back to our lab, we'll have a better—"

A shrill whinny cut her off. She spun in her saddle to find Rumble rearing up with his forehoofs striking the air. Cade wrestled with the colt's head, trying to get him down. The animal dropped to all fours and the loose stone gave way underneath him. Man and wild-eyed horse began to slide down the slope, right toward her. "Ally, look out!"

With her arms still half in her sleeves, she struggled to get Smoky out of the way. Rumble neighed again. From the corner of her eye, she saw him flatten his ears and lunge toward them as if he were escaping a pack of wolves. She saw the hard line of Cade's grim mouth a split second before Rumble hit them.

Slam. The impact drove the breath from her lungs. Gasping, pinned between the horses, Ally felt Smoky start to tumble. The gelding snorted and strove for his footing. A blazing snap of pain raced up her leg as her foot twisted in the stirrup.

The steel band of Cade's arm shot around her middle and plucked her off Smoky's back. The gelding went down with a squeal and the rattle of cascading stones filled her ears.

Cade hauled her over his saddle with one hand and fought to keep Rumble upright with the other. "You all right?" he called over the noise of spilling gravel and whuffing horses.

She tried to speak, but no sound came. The colt's muscles bunched underneath her and he sat so hard on his hindquarters she felt her feet scrape the ground. The world stopped spinning. Somehow they stood firm on the slope again.

Her lungs expanded at last and she sucked in a huge, grateful breath of mountain air, uncaring about the saddle horn jabbing into her belly. Yards below, Smoky lurched to his feet and stood there trembling.

"Ally. Talk to me!" Cade said from somewhere above her head.

"Yuh," she grunted out, unable to say anything more.

Cade walked his colt toward Smoky. "Whoa. Whoa," he called, catching the shaken gelding's bridle. "Stand." He slipped off the colt's back, tied the gelding's reins to Rumble's saddle strings, and then tethered Rumble to a tree.

Through a swimmy whitish haze, she fixed on Cade's worn boots. Her gaze traveled up his muscular, denim-clad legs to narrow hips and stopped there at eye level. "Are you all right?" he asked again.

Yes. No. Oh, mercy, her head ached. And her ankle—oh, God. Aspirin. Whiskey. Anything.

His hand entered her frame of vision, brushing aside her hair. Light shivered at the corner of her eye. The skin of his palm hummed against her cheek.

She blinked and dragged her head up to focus on his broad chest, and then his face.

His arms came around her again and he lifted her off the colt's back. Mmmmm, warm. Solid. She melted into him and her pain receded. The haze increased.

He knelt and pulled her into his lap. Bending close, he studied her. His breath feathered her face. She gazed at the stubble shadowing his cheeks, and then the heart-fluttering deep green of his eyes. "What's my name?" he asked.

Murphy, she thought. She tried to say it, but all that came out was "Mmmmm." *Kiss me again.* Believing she'd said it aloud, she closed her eyes.

"No-no-no," he said. "Ally, wake up!" Instead of kissing her, he slapped her cheek.

Her eyes sprang open. She tried to scowl, but a streak of red over his shoulder caught her attention. She blinked again and tried to focus, then remembered where she was and what had just happened.

Rumble Seat stood at the side of the trail with Smoky. The colt stood still now, but he rolled his eye back as if he thought something might still be chasing him. A smear of blood trickled down his hindquarter. "He's hurt," she mumbled.

Cade gave a long sigh and his frown relaxed a little. "*You're* hurt." His hands skimmed her body.

"Ma'right," she managed. "Help me sit."

He pulled her up, then continued to run his hands down her legs. Sensual little tingles fired in the nerve endings all over her body...until he reached her ankle. "Ouch!"

He shot her an apologetic look and drew down her sock. Gentle fingers circled her ankle and her heartbeat began thudding. "It doesn't feel broken. Let's get you back to the house." He gathered her into his arms again, lifted her, and then carried her back to the colt.

His gaze landed on the chestnut colt's rump. The blood had run all the way down to the animal's hock. Kincade's body stiffened. When he spoke, his voice had gone hard and angry. "He wasn't spooked. He was hit on purpose."

Chapter Five

Morgan stood over the kitchen sink, scrubbing the breakfast dishes with more vigor than necessary. "They're not back yet," she said. "I'm starting to worry." She rinsed a plate and handed it to Elsa. "I have this bad feeling maybe I was wrong about her helping Cade."

Elsa took the plate in one hand and held her other palm over it. A hot breeze flowed from her fingertips, drying the plate almost at once. "I'm sure they're all right. They just went up into the foothills, didn't they? Morgan, you're spilling water!"

A wave of sudsy water sloshed over the edge of the counter. Frowning, Morgan flicked her hand. The cascade of water stopped short of hitting her clean floor, rose upward, and splashed back into the sink basin. "I'm the one who convinced him to let her stay. What if she only makes things worse?"

"You sound almost as bad as Kincade," Elsa chided. She put the dry plate away and took a dripping bowl from Morgan's hand. "I like her."

"You never see a bad side to anybody." Morgan scrubbed a cup, taking more care this time.

Elsa finished drying the last few dishes and put them away. "This family needs a little optimism," she said.

What their family needed was luck, Morgan thought privately. She hadn't told Cade about the new past-due notice they'd received from the bank yesterday afternoon—just quietly called them up and used some of her dwindling savings to pay what she could on it. It wasn't enough, not by a long shot, but it might keep the bank from jerking their home out from under them for a little longer.

Oh, Cade. She wished he'd said something weeks ago about his power fading out. From what she could tell, none of the others, including herself, had experienced any such loss of power. She'd deal with it if that day came, but she worried more how Cade would handle it if his power never returned. He took far too much upon himself, as he always did.

She often thought their presence around the ranch only hindered him. During their teenage years, she'd teased him by calling him "Atlas," bearing the twin weights of their secret and their welfare. He still acted as if he alone were responsible for their safety. She couldn't recall the last time she'd heard a real laugh out of him. They needed to shake things up a bit.

"I have a brilliant idea," she said. She turned on her heel and beamed at Elsa. "We're all going on a picnic this weekend after Sunday service."

Elsa's eyes went round. "What? The park picnic?" They hadn't attended one of Sagerton Community Church's post-service potlucks since Cade dated Maryanne. In fact, Cade and Maryanne's relationship had ended the very last time they tried mingling with the people of Sagerton at one of the park picnics. *Face it,* Ethan had said of the townspeople. *We can keep trying all we want. We'll never be them.*

"Let's see," Morgan said, tapping a short fingernail on the counter. "We can make a peach cobbler, and maybe a pan of lasagna..."

"You know Kincade isn't going to go for that," Elsa warned.

"Go for what?"

Morgan and Elsa turned toward the voice. Kincade's broad shoulders filled the space of the front hall. He entered the greatroom carrying

Allyson in his arms.

At once, all kinds of horrible images sped through Morgan's mind. The tinfoil taste of fear filled her mouth as she remembered the threatening note he had received. She dropped the dishcloth on her clean floor and hurried toward him. "What happened?"

Ally's eyelids fluttered open as he laid her on the couch. "She'll be all right," he said. "She twisted her ankle falling off of Smoky. Elsa, get some aspirin and ice."

The woman's pale brow wrinkled and she frowned up at him. Her lips parted, but he cut her off and added, "Morgan, call Ethan on his cell. Have him ride up to the mountains and take a look around."

"Cade, don't you think—" Ally started to say.

"You'll be fine," he said, sitting on the couch beside her. He brushed a lock of her hair off her face, surprising Morgan. Cade rarely showed open affection, and never with someone he'd only known a couple of days. What on earth had happened this morning?

Elsa returned with the ice pack and aspirin, and he sent her out to look after their horses. Ally took the tablets and swallowed them down with a cup of water.

"All right," Morgan demanded when Elsa had gone. "What are you hiding?"

"Someone followed us into the mountains and spooked our horses," he explained. "And last night, someone broke into the barn and attacked Allyson."

Morgan felt her mouth drop open. So that was why Ally had been on the couch this morning. She planted her hands on her hips. "Why are you just telling me this now?"

"She'll be all right," he said. "There was no reason to scare Elsa with the details." His gaze flicked toward Allyson, who had sat up and begun pressing ginger fingers to her ankle.

Morgan saw a darkening bruise around the puffy joint just before the woman reapplied the ice pack. The soup of nerves in her belly congealed into a solid mass. "Elsa's a big girl now, and so am I."

He drew a deep breath. They'd been through this sort of argument so many times, both could practically recite their lines by rote. "I know that, Morgan," he said in the expected weary tone. "We didn't see a reason to wake you last night just to worry you."

"And how about now?"

"I've got it covered."

Morgan groaned. "You've got to quit thinking you have to protect us. Don't you think we need to know what's going on around here? Especially considering that note?"

Oh, no. Morgan struggled not to clap a hand over her mouth.

Allyson's gaze locked with her own. "What note?"

Looking pained, Cade sighed.

"I have a right to know," Allyson went on when no one replied. "I want this job, but I'm not willing to risk my life for it. Tell me what's going on." Her sharp gray stare shifted back and forth between them.

Well, nothing to be done about it. Morgan couldn't take back what she'd said. Stuffing her guilt into the bottom of her belly with the mass of nerves, she fixed her brother with a hard look. *Please don't blow this chance,* she thought, wishing he could hear her. She gave him an apologetic frown and retreated. "I'll be out with Elsa."

She couldn't begin to guess how he would answer Ally's question, but she prayed he'd say something that would smooth over the redheaded woman's doubts without giving too much away. Not for her own sake. Not even for Ethan or Elsa. Cade needed that woman more than he knew, needed to learn to accept help even if he'd been forced to do so. Maybe Allyson could convince him that he didn't need to hold up their world all by himself.

****

Cade rubbed his face. Stubble scratched his palm. He ignored it.

He had the perfect excuse to tell Allyson he didn't need her. Someone obviously wanted her to fail in her mission at Hope Creek, and they were willing to hurt her to scare her off. He couldn't let her stay and risk life and limb to help him.

Problem was, he didn't want her to go. He rubbed his fingers over his lips, remembering the way her mouth had felt on his. Hell, she'd even *tasted* like strawberry. His manhood stirred at the memory, and he forced the dangerous thoughts back.

"Let me make us something to eat," he barked. He stalked into the kitchen, where he busied himself putting together steak sandwiches out of the previous night's leftovers. She didn't speak, but he felt the full weight of her stare as though she were the Grand Inquisitor.

He brought her the food and they ate in silence. As the minutes ticked by, he sensed her nearing the edge of an outburst. She stared at him with those penetrating eyes and an expectant look on her face.

He stuffed the last of his sandwich into his mouth and chewed with slow deliberation, putting off the unpleasantness until the last minute. Finally, he washed the food down with a gulp of lemonade. "What else would you need to do, now that you've got all your samples?"

Her lips curved downward. She shifted her ice pack to a better spot on her ankle. "I've got to get the results back from the lab, and then I'll know more. Is

65

that what the note was about? Did my department pull this assignment?" Color filled her cheeks.

"No," he answered, staring at the way the early-afternoon sunshine poured through the windows and burnished her hair into silken flame. Why couldn't he just tell her what he was and have it over with? Not just an Elemental, but a non-functioning Elemental. She'd think he was crazy. Didn't make much difference if he spun any wild yarn he wanted. It all ended up the same. He was busted. Useless.

Except with her. When he kissed her, he'd felt such a skin-sizzling surge of power that he had to believe she felt it, too. That would have led to a lot of uncomfortable questions, and he almost didn't care. The heat of her lips had driven him right to the brink. He'd nearly lost his grip on the power, unfamiliar and so much stronger than he remembered it.

He wanted it back. All of it, but especially the feel of her body molded against his.

She pressed the ice pack to her ankle and winced. Guilt swept everything else out of his head. "Your ankle's not broken," he said, "but you shouldn't be up on it for a few days. I think it would be best if you went back to Bozeman."

When she looked up, the hurt pride on her face knifed him in the belly. "You're kicking me out?"

He turned toward the coffee table to avoid that expression on her face. "It's not that I don't think you can help me," he said. "You'll be safer back at the university."

She stared so hard, he felt her gaze burning on his skin. "You need me."

She meant he needed her botanical skills, but his body reacted with a zap of hunger. He laid his palms on his dusty jeans, forcing himself to sit still instead of grabbing her and kissing her again. He sucked in a deep breath. Big mistake. A whiff of strawberries tortured him.

With a supreme effort, he dragged his attention to her injury. He found it easier to focus on the ice pack than the tantalizing scent of her hair, but not by much. The spine-bending weight of responsibility settled on his shoulders. He shouldn't have ridden into the mountains with her, not after that note. He should have called the sheriff in the first place, but then he'd have to explain what the writer thought Cade had to hide. Allyson would be all right. Thank God for that.

The horses had suffered worse. They'd ridden double on the colt back to the ranch, leading the injured gelding behind. The feel of her curvy rear snuggled between his thighs, and the almost-embrace of keeping his arm around her to take the reins, had been exquisite agony the entire way.

Both animals would recover, but Cade hated losing them when it came time to ride fence or get the herd in and out of the pasture. They had few enough good horses already, since he'd had to sell many of them, and lost others in the barn fire.

He worried still more about the film in his head stuck on Replay. He kept seeing the terrified look on Ally's face when she was wedged between a couple thousand pounds of tumbling horse. Again, he had to command his body not to close the space between them.

"Kincade."

Realizing he'd been silent for several moments, he mustered words to thrust between them. "If you're just waiting for lab results, maybe it's better you go back to the university."

Her eyes speared him. "A fall from a horse isn't going to stop me from finishing this assignment. I've got a job to do and a livelihood to protect, same as you. What makes you think I'm giving up on day two?"

He watched her struggle to elevate her foot and still keep the ice pack on it. With a sigh, he sat on the coffee table and arranged the pillows for her. "Ally, this wasn't an accident. Someone doesn't want you here. My horse had a puncture wound. Not a sting, not a snake bite."

"I will not lose my job."

"You'd rather lose your life?"

"This assignment means everything to me," she said, "and it isn't just lab results and computer formulas. I have to be here to test the environment. Prevailing winds, local plant life and insect species, rainfall—"

"Well, as you can see, it isn't raining." He ran a hand through his hair and started to get up.

Her hand came down on his thigh and cemented him in place. "You don't understand. I need this. I could get a research appointment." She met his gaze with an expression that tugged at him, at once hopeful and resolute. "I want to finish this job."

What would she say if she knew what stood in her way of the appointment was him? For a moment, he pictured working with her to find a solution. Even if his power didn't come back, maybe they could do something that would help him to keep his ranch, and her to get that research position.

No. Her life was more important than a job, even one that seemed to mean so much to her. And he didn't need another person's life in his hands.

"You can't stay," he said. He rose to his feet, letting her palm slide off his leg. "I'll write you whatever references—"

"You can't seriously be turning me down." Ice pack forgotten, Ally shifted as though planning to spring to her feet as well. "What about your agreement with Doctor Coonan? Are you going to take back your offer of a field lab for the students, too?"

"I am the one who wrote the letter requesting help. I have every right to rescind that request, and my offer, if I don't think your work is doing any good."

Her voice caught in a squawk of outrage. "We've barely started!"

"And now we're finished."

Pillows tumbled to the floor. She wrestled to her feet and balanced there one-legged. "I have the chance one day of getting research funding that could help us find new answers to crop-farming problems. No one's going to give me that chance unless I get my foot in the door first."

"You see what happened when you got your foot in my door," he growled, gesturing to her injury. "No job is worth your life, Ally."

"I'll work under your watch. Or Ethan's, or Elsa's—"

"They can't be spared. We don't have a lot of hands on this ranch, and we need every one to keep it running." He grimaced at the unpleasant taste of the words on his lips. Once upon a time, his power and one or two strong backs had been all the ranch needed to flourish. Now, he and his brother and sisters worked longer and harder than ever, only to watch Hope Creek slipping into disrepair.

"If an extra worker is all you need, I'll help." Ally planted her hands on her hips, somehow imposing even with that wayward hair and stork-legged stance. A hint of strawberries floated past his nose again.

Forcing himself not to inhale too deeply, he asked, "How are you going to help with a sprained ankle?"

She hobbled closer. The light touch of her hands on his forearms branded his skin. "Please let me stay."

More than anything she'd said so far, those four

words struck him in their simplicity. His head swam with her sweet scent and the earnest entreaty in her eyes. What the hell did she see in the place that made it worth sticking around? There had to be a million easier assignments, a million better places to be.

He looked away, only to fix on the generous curves of her body. Her breasts rose and fell through the thin material of her shirt. The feel of her fingers curled around his arms vibrated into the pit of his belly, and all at once he ached to pull her against him. He took a step forward and pulled her hands away from his arms. Forcing a gruff tone, he said, "Sit back down. You need to ice that ankle."

"At least tell me whether or not you're going to let me finish my work here," she said, pinning him with her stare.

His blood simmered. Oh, he wanted her to finish something, all right. The smell of her, and that uncompromising look in her eyes, drew him toward her like a gravitational pull. Still holding her hands, he stepped forward again and kissed her.

Power surged in his blood, bubbling from the center outward to the tips of his fingers, down his legs, and into his feet. He almost broke the kiss, but then she curled her arms up around his neck and leaned against him. She moaned against his lips and cupped his face with her silk-soft hands.

Oh, hell. Throwing the last of his conscious protests aside, he slanted his mouth over hers and let himself drown in her. His skin buzzed with the unmistakable sign of his gift, but now he couldn't bring himself to care. She tasted too good, smelled so incredible... Could he make this last forever?

Thumping boots echoed in the front hallway. Ally broke the kiss first, looking as startled as he. She stepped back, then yelped and collapsed to the couch.

Cade bent to help her, still fighting the throbbing buzz echoing throughout his body. He seized the ice pack in one hand and cupped her slender ankle with the other. The contact of her cool skin against his burning palm slammed his senses into overdrive again. *Kiss her kiss her kiss her,* taunted the devil on his shoulder. He stared into her eyes, and it seemed she was pulling him toward her again with a mere look...

"Checked out the mountain trail on my way back to the house," said Ethan as he entered the greatroom. "Morgan said Allyson was hurt."

Mustering his scattered thoughts, Cade said, "She'll be all right."

Ethan removed his cowboy hat to scratch his shaggy head. His gaze flicked from Ally to Cade and back again with a knowing air that sandpapered under Cade's skin. "You need anything, Miss Hamilton?"

Lines appeared in her brow. "Bailey," she said. "He's been cooped up all day. I've got to get him—"

"I'll worry about Bailey. I'll give him a good run tonight," Cade broke in, seeing the unhappy look on her face. "You rest that ankle, and we'll see about your work in the morning."

Her gaze shot back to him. "You're not telling me to go?"

"I'm not saying anything yet. You've invested a lot of time so far—"

"I'll say," interrupted Ethan. "Looks like y'all been busy all day up there in the foothills. What'd you do, back up a truck straight from the greenhouse?"

Cade swiveled around to eye his foster brother. "What are you talking about?"

Ethan's brows lifted. With a shrug, he said, "The whole trail about a mile up is covered in wild sunflowers."

****

Using a carved antique cane Elsa had fished from storage, Ally hobbled to the front porch and lowered herself into a wooden rocker. She'd been stewing since dinner, shifting back and forth between confusion and annoyance.

How had wildflowers popped into existence on a trail that had been barren two hours before? Was someone playing tricks on her?

There hadn't been time to ask Kincade about it. As soon as Ethan got back, he whisked his older brother away to round up the livestock for evening feed. Cade mumbled something about talking later, and then hurried off as if she'd breathed fire at him.

Men.

Elsa came out onto the porch, then slid a footstool toward the rocker and laid a pillow on it for Ally's injured ankle. She ducked back inside and emerged again with a glass of iced tea. Setting it on the table beside the chair, she asked, "Do you need anything else?"

Summoning a preoccupied smile, Ally replied, "I'm all right, thanks." Elsa didn't look fooled, so Ally pulled her mini-recorder from her shirt pocket. "Lots of work to do."

"I've got work to do in the horse barn myself," said Elsa. "Call down there if you need me." She laid the cordless phone beside Ally's tea. With a grin, the young woman jogged down the treadworn wooden steps toward the barn.

Ally watched the woman go. A walking ray of sunshine, that one. She'd probably be first in line to save the world if she could manage it.

Shaking her head, Ally opened her notebook and muttered, "I'd settle for saving my job."

She skimmed a fingertip down the list of figures in her notebook. She'd recorded all the preliminary soil data she could gather with on-site equipment.

Frowning, she pressed a button on her recorder. "Soil pH is normal," she said into the device. "Nutrient concentration is optimal, according to first field tests. No apparent insect damage, no over- or under-irrigation. Pasture doesn't appear to be overgrazed."

She clicked off the recorder and ran a hand through her wayward bangs. Staring into the paddock across the driveway, she studied the short, yellowing grasses. How could the numbers look like this, and his fields look like *that*? Maybe tomorrow, she could talk him into testing a section of his land with various fertilizers. Pawn it off as a project for the university students, since they'd be using his ranch as a field lab this fall.

Elsa had brought her a box of files from her bunk in the horse barn, as well as a folder containing notes from Hope Creek's previous owners. From what Ally could tell, the elderly couple hadn't had much trouble keeping the ranch in the black. The place almost ran itself, turning out crop after crop of foals that brought an eyebrow-raising price at auction, not to mention the money they made on beefers.

"Then what changed?" she mused, tapping a chewed pencil against her lips. Her thoughts kept wandering back to chemicals in the soil, but Cade was so adamantly opposed to them that she couldn't imagine that being the case.

Lab tests, she scribbled into the notebook margin. Then she underlined it twice. Numbers never lied. So either her data was wrong, or something would turn up when she got the results back from the university. Something *had* to.

She noticed the passage of time only when the porch light flickered on. When she looked up again, the sun had disappeared behind the horse barn and the air had cooled. Crickets began to replace the symphony of birdsong.

Cade strode toward her across the driveway carrying Bailey in his arms. The moment the pup saw her he barked and began thrashing to get down.

Cade thumped up the porch steps and set Bailey on his feet. The pup plopped his forepaws on Ally's leg and stretched his nose toward her face, tongue lapping at the air.

Laughing, Ally scooped him up. The dog wriggled, covering her cheek with slobbering kisses. She nuzzled his velvety ear, inhaling the homey scent of fresh straw and something sweet. Drawing back, she saw a reddish smudge on his ear. "What did you get into?"

"Morgan's raspberry preserves. He knocked a bottle off a shelf in the bunkroom."

"How'd you manage that?" she asked the dog while trying to fend off his over-exuberant attentions. "Did someone get you a stepladder?"

Cade scratched the back of his neck, then broke into a grin. "I was carrying him around. Couldn't find his new leash."

Ally set Bailey down and he flopped onto the floorboards at the foot of her chair. "You took my dog for a walk and carried him the whole way?"

"I promised I'd walk him, didn't I?"

Fighting laughter, she studied Cade. He kept right on grinning until that damned dimple appeared in his cheek, setting her insides on frappé. What sort of man was he, anyway? The minute she thought she'd figured him out, he...well, he walked her dog without actually walking him.

"Look, it's getting late," he said. "Why don't you come in the house for a coffee?" he asked. "Bailey can come, too."

For a second, she thought she hadn't heard him right. After all the guff he'd given her about the dog, that was a sure one-eighty. He held her gaze, all innocence.

Yeah, right.

Then she remembered her fertilizer plan. Well, no better time to hit him with it, since he was in such a generous mood already. She beamed. "That's perfect. I need to talk to you about using a section of your land for testing." Shifting her weight onto the cane, she stood up.

"What kind of testing?" he asked.

"Fertilizers." Seeing his expression darken, she added, "Don't get all worried. It'll be a small piece of land, not even an acre. For a control experiment. My initial numbers came back fine for soil nutrients, but that doesn't mean something funny isn't going on out there."

Something funny, indeed. Visions of sunflowers flashed through her head, followed by absurd images of Cade sneaking into the mountains and planting them without her knowledge.

But when? How? Why?

He pierced her with that cryptic stare. Tiny shivers rippled through her body from the center out. His gaze lowered to her lips.

Her heartbeat stumbled and resumed at double speed. She struggled to keep from leaning toward him for another kiss. The one on the mountain trail, and the second in the house, had been only a taste. A tantalizing promise of the wonderful things he could do with that mouth. The ache of her injured ankle ceased to be as she swam in those jewel-green eyes.

His broad shoulders lifted once. "All right, fine. You get the garden," he said.

She blinked and came back to reality. "Oh. Okay. That'll be..." What had they been talking about just now?

His dimple returned and a deep chuckle rumbled up from his chest. "You're welcome. Let's go in. C'mon, Bailey."

The dog woofed and led the way to the door. Cade followed. "This way, Miss Hamilton."

Bailey trotted inside as if he'd been expecting the invitation since their arrival on the ranch. Ally hobbled forward on her cane, puzzled by Cade's turnaround but too distracted by that sexy dimple to keep her mind on soil tests and botany.

She entered the house, feeling his gaze on her the whole way down the front hall. Lord, even his stare made her want to jump into his arms.

Chapter Six

Morgan was folding laundry on the table when Kincade and Ally entered the kitchen. He expected his sister to comment on Bailey's presence indoors, but she went back to hanging a pair of Ethan's jeans on a hanger. "Maryanne called again," she said. "She's coming over to talk with you about Jim."

Cade and Ally sat down. Frowning, he picked up a banana from the bowl on the table and began peeling it. "What about him?" he asked.

"She didn't say," answered Morgan. "She'll be here in an hour, and you can ask her yourself."

A few moments later, Ethan strolled into the kitchen. "What's to eat?"

Morgan finished folding a shirt. "Dinner was two hours ago."

"Yeah. I'm hungry," he said.

Swiping a hanger at him, Morgan demanded, "What am I, your personal chef? The minute I make something, you've eaten it. You drive me nuts."

"You love me. I love your food." Ethan hooked a pear from the fruit bowl and crunched into it.

Morgan shook her head, but Cade saw the telltale smile of satisfaction tugging at her lips. Sometimes he thought their sister's cooking was the only reason Ethan stayed at Hope Creek. Cade popped a chunk of banana into his mouth and chewed.

He hadn't heard much from Maryanne since their breakup months ago. This week, she seemed to be a burr clinging to his shirt. Jim must be in worse health than he'd thought. Bad luck all around, these days.

But Cade's luck might be changing. He studied the banana's bright yellow skin, thinking of the sunflowers on the mountain trail. Scads of them, Ethan had said. Little things yet, just beginning to flower. So fast. He itched to get up there and survey the patch of wildflowers, even though the sun was setting and the mountains would soon be cloaked in blue-black darkness.

He stole a look at Ally, only to be arrested by those piercing gray eyes. The minute he locked gazes with her, she turned away to stare at the table and her expression went blank. Did she suspect anything of his gift?

How could she know? He and his family were glitches in the system, walking freaks of nature that shouldn't be. Unless she sidelined on tabloid television shows, powers like his couldn't have occurred to her.

Maybe that searching look was meant to accuse him of playing pranks on her. He *was* responsible for the sunflowers. He thought. He hoped. Just not the way she figured.

Could she restore his gift? He struggled to peel his attention away from her. What if something in *him* was responding to something in *her*?

What if she left before he could get his power back?

Not gonna happen, growled the devil on his shoulder, and for once he agreed with it. He couldn't let her go, not now. But how could he keep her here long enough to know if she was the answer?

Mess up her research, the devil answered at once.

His belly clenched. The very idea of deceiving her when she'd already proven herself so determined to help him save Hope Creek...

No. Unthinkable.

Yes, taunted the devil. *Do you want to lose your home? Your family's home?*

His snack settled like a cannonball in his stomach. Just tampering with her research wouldn't be enough. She could rewrite lost notes. He wouldn't even be able to get his hands on some of the data anyway, since it was already on its way to the lab to be logged. He'd have to get under her skin. Distract her. Tempt her away from her many books and little glass vials.

Seduce her.

He shot out of the chair, stalked across the kitchen, then pitched the rest of his banana into the trash. "Gotta take a shower," he said.

"Cade, didn't you want—" she said behind him.

Forcing himself to keep walking, he pretended not to hear her. He shoved open his bedroom door and let it bang shut behind him.

Exhaling harshly, he leaned back against the door. His gut twisted at the thought of lying to her and interfering with her job—maybe even her coveted promotion—by losing her notes or confusing her data. But the idea of seducing her...

He wanted that part.

Christ. Even something as simple and honest as desire had to be tainted with guilt. He needed his gift. He'd already let his family down by cursing them with their powers in the first place. But hell. He couldn't just want the woman without feeling the familiar old mantle of blame snuggling around his shoulders.

Brooding and resentful, he stripped out of his shirt and jeans as he walked through the bathroom. He tossed the clothing into the laundry basket in his walk-in closet.

Stepping into the shower, he let the hot water slide over his skin and breathed in the steam and humid air. None of it helped.

Screw it. She was an adult. He was an adult. She'd made no secret of her own desires.

"All right. Be dishonest, you stupid sonofabitch," he grumbled to his reflection in the shaving mirror. He wiped water out of his eyes and swept his damp locks back.

He remembered her strawberry smell and silky skin, and bit back a groan. Did it count as dishonesty if, somewhere under all that misguided motivation, he really did want the woman in his bed?

After finishing his shower, he pulled on a pair of navy-blue jogging pants and a gray T-shirt. He stuffed all the nagging bullshit down into his belly and slapped a lid on it, then found an easygoing smile from some other, more detached part of him. He re-entered the kitchen scrubbing a towel in his dripping hair. Ethan had disappeared. "Sorry," Cade said. "A man can take just so much barn dust."

Morgan stared hard at him, looking not the least convinced. He steered his smile away from her and onto Ally. "How about that coffee?"

"Sure," she answered, still eyeing him as if she thought he were hiding something.

Well, he was...sort of.

Bailey lay beside her chair thumping his tail against the floor. Cade bent to scratch the pup's ears, then went to the coffeepot to brew a batch.

"Did you mean it about the garden?" Ally asked.

"Yeah," he said. "That patch of land won't make much difference in the bigger scheme of things, so I guess you can do whatever you want with it. It can't get any more dead."

"Thank you so much for the vote of confidence." Her mouth quirked up at one corner and her slender reddish eyebrows drew together.

He grinned back, and was gratified to see her gaze shift away to the table. He chose not to acknowledge Morgan's sharp look as his sister finished the laundry and carried it off to the bedrooms.

He brought a pair of filled mugs to the table and plunked one in front of Ally. "How's the ankle?"

"All right, if I'm not on it," she replied. "It won't stop me from working." She sipped her coffee.

"Good." Her lashes fluttered and a faint line appeared between her brows. She hadn't expected that—and small wonder. He'd done nothing but slow her progress since her arrival. A little weird to hear him start championing her now, he supposed. Points for throwing her off balance.

He reached into a jar on the kitchen counter, extracted a handful of foil-wrapped chocolates, then dropped all but one on the table. He adopted his best expression of nonchalance, sat beside her, and began unwrapping the chocolate he'd kept. "Have some."

"No, thanks." Skepticism filled her tone.

"C'mon," he prodded. "Morgan orders them special from New York. Best chocolate in the country."

After a moment, she shrugged and reached for the pile of chocolates. "Do you intend to ply me with coffee and sweets? I'm already planning to help you."

"I intend you to sit back, rest that ankle, and enjoy yourself for the night."

She popped a morsel of chocolate between her lips, which then curved into a smile. Her eyes closed and she raised her chin. Her hair slid back, exposing the slender curve of her throat. No baking in the sun for Ally Hamilton. Her skin was smooth and pale, and glowed like porcelain so delicate that a beam of sunlight could have shone right through it. "Mmmm," she moaned. "These *are* good."

"Morgan knows food, all right," he said, riveted on that creamy skin. He fought the urge to lean forward, press his lips to it, and discover if it was as soft as it looked. To keep his mouth busy, he stuffed the truffle into it and gulped it down, then chased it with a swallow of coffee that burned his throat. Coughing until his eyes watered, he surged out of the chair to get a glass of cool water.

"Are you all right?" she asked.

He sucked down half a glass of water before he could reply. When he trusted himself to speak, he answered, "How about some TV?"

"You've been very strange this evening, Kincade."

"Strange how?"

She raised her hands into the air. "You've been looking at me like I've grown a second head, and now, you're standing as far across the room as you can get from me."

He looked behind him and realized that he stood by the refrigerator, almost all the way back toward the never-used formal dining room. Chagrin flashed through him. He shoved it aside and stalked back toward the kitchen table, adopting an air of overconfidence that would have made Ethan proud. Sitting in his chair again, he leaned toward Ally and propped his elbows on his knees. "Is this better, Miss Hamilton?"

An intriguing rosy blush colored her cheeks. The pulse at her throat sped up and he fixed on it, imagining his mouth pressed against the skin there. He leaned closer and her lips parted slightly. "I'm not sure we should be..."

"What's the matter? We've kissed," he said. He allowed a smile to tug at his lips.

She angled her head. "If I remember right, you were the one to stop that. A bad idea. Your words, Cade, not mine."

Damn. For a moment, he thought about backing away, but the devil on his shoulder jabbed him and he stayed put. He managed to keep the smile on his face. "Maybe I had a change of heart."

She frowned. "What do you want from me?"

Her strawberry scent drifted to his nose then. Instead of avoiding it this time, he leaned a fraction closer, inhaled deeply, and let her see him do it. "What is it?" he murmured. "Shampoo? Soap? You smell incredible."

Her color heightened. "Body lotion."

He raked her with his gaze, imagining spreading the stuff over her porcelain skin. He didn't bother disguising his interest. Now that he'd made all his excuses to seduce her, he decided, to hell with his baggage. If a man had to do a thing, he did it thoroughly.

Not that he needed much encouragement on that. He stared at her mouth and leaned close enough to feel her fast, shallow breath on his face. "About that kiss," he said, hovering just over her lips.

"What?" she asked, her voice husky. Her eyes softened with a silvery glow of desire that went straight to his groin.

He forced himself to stay still, prolonging the moment when he wanted only to pull her into his lap and give her mouth a thorough exploration. "I might need a reminder of what I turned down," he drawled.

The tip of her tongue flitted across her lips and he couldn't wait another minute. Growling softly, he captured her mouth with his own.

A faint moan escaped her and her lips parted.

His body blazed. He plunged his tongue into her mouth, tasting chocolate and coffee and Allyson, all rolled into one unique flavor that he could have lived on for the rest of his life. With his manhood straining for release, he wondered who was seducing who. She tasted so damn good that he forgot he should have been testing for his power, until a cool voice cut in with, "I hope I'm not interrupting."

****

Allyson sat upright so fast her chair skidded backward. Her feet smacked the floor, sending sparks of pain up her leg from her injured ankle.

Bailey woofed and sprang to his feet. Allyson grabbed his collar. The dog hovered beside her, twitching with eagerness to investigate their visitors.

A woman stood in the entrance hallway staring at them. She approached with a confident, hip-swinging stride that made it plain she owned any room into which she walked. In a white silk top, jeans, and expensive-looking boots, she sure dressed the part. Ally doubted those boots ever saw a speck of mud.

Behind her came the man Ally remembered seeing in town with Brady Hart—the stylish male equivalent to the woman before her now. Even in jeans and an oxford shirt, he looked too sophisticated for Cade's relaxed, rustic greatroom. He cast a studious look around as he followed the woman toward the kitchen table.

The woman angled her head and studied Ally. Her chunky black curls bounced with the motion, exposing a pair of diamond earrings so large they couldn't have been missed by a blind man.

At once Ally knew who this was, but the woman extended a bejeweled hand. "Maryanne Sagerton. And you are...?"

"Allyson Hamilton. How do you do?" Ally heard herself say. Half of her registered the cool, manicured hand that slid into her own, while the other half fizzed with residual tension from Cade's kiss. She made herself smile.

"I could die for a latte," Maryanne said, smoothing a hand over her glossy curls. She pivoted on her heel and smiled at Kincade, exuding warmth. "I hope you don't mind we let ourselves in."

Cade's brow lifted in what Ally had begun to think of as his bullshit-detector expression. He rose from his chair and held a hand out to the man. "Cade Murphy."

"Paul Riegel, Maryanne's fiancé," the man responded. "Listen, I parked my car in front of the porch. Is that a good spot?"

"It's fine," answered Cade, sounding like he did mind but didn't want to waste time arguing the point. "No latte. Coffee?"

"That would be great," answered Paul. He shook Ally's hand. "I see you've had a mishap," he added, gesturing to her bandaged ankle.

"Something like that." Ally scratched behind Bailey's ears, then released him.

The pup trotted straight to Paul and began sniffing at his pricey leather shoes. He rose onto his hindlegs, looking like he was about to plant his dusty paws on Paul's jeans.

She grabbed for Bailey's collar and pulled him back. The pup gave a disappointed whine and sat beside her, tail thumping the hardwood floor. "Sorry, he still has a few things to learn about proper greetings."

Paul bent down, wrinkling creases in his jeans that Ally was sure had been ironed there. He patted Bailey's head. "No problem. I've had a few dogs in my time, Miss Hamilton."

Maryanne drifted toward the kitchen counter, where Cade was scooping coffee grounds into a filter. She murmured something close to his ear and an unwanted frisson of jealousy skittered through Ally.

Cade finished brewing the coffee and brought a pair of mugs back to the table. Maryanne followed with two more. "Dad's not doing well at all," she said. She spoke in a low, intimate tone, as though only she and Cade were in the room.

Her fiancé sat on Ally's far side at the end of the

table. He gazed out the greatroom windows at the expansive field beyond the house, looking unconcerned with the way Maryanne seemed to hover at Cade's shoulder. Ally hid a frown. *He's got more confidence in her than I do.*

Maryanne drew out the chair beside Ally and sat down, effectively forcing Cade to sit on her other side. For a moment, Ally wondered if the woman had intended to plant herself between them, but the worry shading Maryanne's pale blue eyes spun threads of doubt within her. After all, she would have worried at least as much about her own father, if he'd been in the hospital.

"What do you do, Miss Hamilton?" Paul asked, breaking into her conflicting thoughts.

She smiled. "I'm a botanist. How about you?"

"Real estate," he answered, then gave an answering grin that crinkled his eyes at the corners. "Not looking for a new house, are you?"

Ally smiled. It was easy to see why Maryanne had been attracted to the man. "Nope. Sorry."

"You win some, you lose some."

"What's the matter with Jim?" Cade asked Maryanne. "I thought the doctors had patched him up."

Sighing, Maryanne traced a finger along the handle of her coffee mug. "Daddy refuses to take his medications and the ulcer just keeps coming back," she said. "You know him. He won't stop eating all that spicy, greasy food, and now that Mom's not around, I can't keep him in line. He says I'm a harpy."

Cade chuckled. "Ornery cuss never did like taking direction." His gaze slid toward Ally. She thought she saw him wink at her and it warmed her insides into a pudding. Then he turned his attention back to Maryanne, and Ally saw a little of his exasperation return. "What do you want me to do?"

"Talk to him," Maryanne said. "He always listened to you."

His gaze flicked toward Paul then, and Ally wondered whether Jim Sagerton ever listened to his future son-in-law. Probably not, since Maryanne was here begging her ex for help.

With a sigh, Cade raised his coffee mug to his lips. "I'll see what I can do."

"Thanks, Cade. I knew I could count on you." Maryanne pushed her chair out and stood. "I see you've done some work on the old horse barn. Mind showing us around?"

Ally saw a muscle work in his jaw as he responded, "Elsa can do it. She's in the new barn right now. Ally shouldn't be on her feet."

Maryanne turned to Ally with an expression that implied she'd forgotten anyone else was in the room. "You don't mind, do you?"

To Ally's dismay, she found she did mind. She and Cade had been right in the middle of—her cheeks grew warm—possibly the most amazing kiss ever. Even their first one hadn't been as good. Did kissing him just get better and better each time? And if it did, what about...other things? A tantalizing shiver spread through her at the possibilities.

She noticed Maryanne still looking at her and forced her thoughts away from those tempting distractions. How embarrassing, with everyone right here in the room, and her thinking about— "Not at all!" she said, so loudly that Maryanne flinched. "You three go ahead. I have coffee to finish and a garden to plan, and I'll be cozy right there on the couch."

Hopefully with Cade later this evening...

"Go, go!" Ally said. She got up and her ankle screamed in protest, but she forced a smile. "Look around, take your time."

Oh, I love how he took his time kissing me...

"Shoo," she added, then snatched her notebook from the table.

"I'll catch up," said Cade. Maryanne and Paul moved toward the front hall. Their voices faded and Ally heard the front door open.

Cade's gaze shifted to her and goose bumps raced over her arms. Ooh, that look would get her in trouble. She wondered if her sinful thoughts of him showed on her face.

Oh, yes, they did. His mouth twitched and his dimple appeared. Ally felt her ears burn, but Cade's stare rendered them icy by comparison with other places on her body. He stood up with such a heated look that she had to fight the urge to step toward him.

She needn't have bothered. He closed the distance with a sweeping step. "I don't think we were finished."

Her mouth went dry. Without thinking, she skimmed her lips with her tongue. Cade swooped down and kissed her.

The moment his lips touched hers, something buzzed in her ears, and this time it couldn't be explained away by insects. She broke the kiss. "What *is* that?"

His eyes clouded. Guilt screamed from every line of his rigid posture. "What's what?"

"Don't give me that," she said. "Something funny's going on."

He frowned and backed away a step. "Why don't you tell me what it is, then, and we'll both know?"

"Cade, I'm not stupid."

"No one said—" he began.

"Stop," she demanded. "Just tell me why you're looking at me like you've swallowed a canary. It's not the first time you've looked like that, either."

A smile curled across his face once more and he

moved back toward her. The spicy tang of cedar wafted through the air. Cologne? Did a guy who worked with horses and cattle all day bother with cologne?

His hand skimmed her arm. A delicious little zing flashed through her. "You've been noticing my looks?" he murmured, a breath away from her lips.

She'd been noticing much more than that. Even the way he filled up a room just by being in it. Frazzled, she pulled her arm away. "That's not what I mean."

Instead of reaching again for her arm, he traced a lock of her hair between his fingertips. "Know what I've noticed?" he asked. He angled his head and gave her a sexy, unhurried appraisal.

"What?" she breathed.

He brushed her lips with his own, a feather touch. Ally's heart pounded loud enough for Idaho to hear it. "I've noticed," he said against her lips, "that you've been here only a couple days now, and I can't seem to stop wanting to kiss you." He lingered on her lower lip, grazing it with his teeth. "Think your department'll consider this harassment?" Another nibbling kiss. "Do *you* consider it harassment? 'Cause I can stop."

Lord, no. She'd hit him with that antique cane if he did. In case he had any such thoughts, she twisted her hands in his shirt and pulled him closer.

Laughter rumbled in his chest. "I was teasing," he said.

You still are, she thought, sinking into another mind-bending kiss.

Until she heard the scream.

Chapter Seven

Cade lunged away from Ally as though he'd been yanked and ran toward the front door. Bailey erupted into an ominous growl. Cade heard a clatter, and then rhythmic thumps behind him. When he looked back over his shoulder, he saw Ally hurrying after him, supported by an old cane. "Stay put."

"Like heck," she said, giving him a mutinous stare. She thumped right along after him even as he threw open the door and ran down the porch steps.

Diablo reared up and pawed the air with his forehoofs, his dark hide shining in the glow of the barn floodlights. The steam-whistle blast of his neigh ricocheted off the barn into the cooling night air. Standing a few yards away in his paddock, Elsa had one hand in the air toward the stallion, and with the other she was trying to push Paul behind her. Her angry shouts floated across the driveway.

Cade rushed across the drive. "What in God's name—" He stopped short when Paul rounded toward the fence and stretched a hand out to help someone up. Maryanne, with her hair in disarray, struggled to her feet. "What happened?" he asked instead.

"That lunatic animal nearly killed my fiancée, is what!" Paul hollered. With a bracing grip on Maryanne's arm, he helped her over the fence and out of the paddock. Three long, energetic strides brought him nose to nose with Cade. "You had better put that animal down, Mister Murphy."

"He wasn't hurting anyone until you two went into his paddock!" yelled Elsa, startling Diablo, who had come down onto all fours and stood shaking beside her.

Maryanne, who hadn't spoken yet, cast a wary look at the stallion. "He was never that mean, Kincade." A hint of accusation laced her voice as if Cade himself had done something to cause Diablo's drastic change.

"Stay out of his paddock and he won't be," Cade snapped. They shouldn't have entered the paddock, Elsa had probably told them that—but Cade felt an unwelcome ooze of responsibility for the accident. Forcing more calm and concern into his tone, he asked Maryanne, "Are you all right?"

She began brushing off her shirt, not looking at him. "I'm fine—"

"What do you mean?" Paul demanded. "I saw that maniac horse kick—"

"He was minding his own business until they went up to him," Elsa interrupted, standing with one hand on the trembling horse's neck. "He didn't even spook until she tried grabbing for his halter." She sounded absurdly proud of the stallion, a fact which might have amused Cade at any other time.

Paul took Maryanne's arm again and thrust it under Cade's nose, ignoring his fiancée's offended look at the way he handled her. In the floodlight glare, Cade saw grass stains, dirt, and a reddish smudge in the torn white silk of her sleeve. "I don't call that minding his own business," snarled Paul.

"An accident, I'm sure," Maryanne said at last, her voice clipped and cool. She withdrew her arm from Paul's grasp and gave Cade a brief, irritated frown. "Let's just go."

She and Paul drifted away to his luxury car, parked just shy of crushing the reedy flowers planted at the base of the porch.

Elsa came to the fence, leading the fractious stallion with gentle murmurs, just as Ally made it to

Cade's side. "What happened?" Ally asked.

"Diablo, of course," Cade answered. He rubbed the back of his neck, wondering what to do. Maryanne would be within her rights to have the horse impounded, even if she had entered his paddock without permission. He turned to Elsa. "What were they doing in there, anyway?"

"I don't know. They were in the barn with me one second, and the next, I turned away to finish the evening feed, and..." She waved a hand at Diablo, who snorted and shied backward.

Ally hobbled up to the fence and reached a hand out, palm up, toward the stallion. Elsa gave her a wary look, but Ally merely held her palm there. The stallion's ears twitched back and forth a few times, and then curiosity won out. He stretched his neck forward as far as possible without having to step closer, and sniffed.

She let the stallion's quivering muzzle skim her palm, and then, so smoothly Cade almost didn't see the point of contact, she slid her palm up the horse's face to rub his glossy black cheek. "You're not such a grouchy old ogre after all, are you?" she murmured. "She just scared you, didn't she, boy?"

The low, musical tone of her words sent intriguing little pulses through Cade's body. He glanced toward the barn, wishing he hadn't fixed the lock after all. She'd have had to stay in the house.

Then he berated himself for the impulsive notion. She had work to do, and he was interfering with her concentration for his own selfish desires. What if she lost her job because of him?

Don't start backtracking now, he thought with a frown. *You got yourself into this mess, Cade Murphy, and you need to finish what you started...or lose this place.*

She turned to him then, and her smile washed all of his doubts away. "I think I'll turn in, if that's all right. I've had enough excitement for one day."

"All right. G'night," Cade said, forcing ease into his tone when he wanted only to kiss her again. The pulses in his body sped up at the mental image of them intertwined, of his mouth tracing that fair, soft skin. Kissing her had become some sort of addiction. The more he did it, the more he wanted to continue doing it. He turned toward the house in what he hoped was a fair show of unconcern, but he thought he saw a flicker of suspicion in Elsa's eyes. "See you in the morning."

His distance from Ally was no easier as he stripped down to a pair of boxer shorts and climbed into bed. With nothing to distract his thoughts, they sped straight to her. He half wanted to get back out of bed and go to her.

Too soon, warned the guilty part of him that wanted his powers back. Rushing her would only scare her off. She wouldn't—

The jangling telephone broke into his thoughts. He picked it up. "Hello?"

"Is this Kincade Murphy?" asked a smooth female voice.

Not recognizing the caller, Cade glanced at the clock on his nightstand. Just about nine p.m. "Yes," he said. "Who's speaking?"

"Mister Murphy, this is Julie Belhurst of the Department of Plant Pathology at Montana State. I'm sorry, I realize I'm calling sort of late. I'm at home right now, trying to work with some of this data Miss Hamilton gave me. She was supposed to have collected some additional information, and I'm afraid I can't proceed without it. If she's there, I really need to speak to her."

A flicker of curiosity and annoyance passed though him, but he managed to keep it out of his tone. "This couldn't wait until morning?"

"I'm a single-minded person in my work, Mister

Murphy, and Doctor Coonan's a bit impatient for the results," she said. He heard the insincere apology in her voice, along with a faint smugness that suggested Ally had come to Hope Creek for a vacation.

"All right," he said, scraping in his nightstand drawer for pencil and paper. "Does she have your home number? I can have her call you."

"Is she not there?" Julie asked, and this time her frosty edge was clearer.

"She's down at the barn. It's a separate line," he answered, making sure she heard the censure in his voice. In the two days she'd been at Hope Creek, Ally had never shown herself to be anything but dedicated to her job. Hell, she'd stayed on after a burglary and a sprained ankle. He hated to think what disasters awaited her for the rest of her stay.

Julie seemed confused about why her botanist colleague would be hanging out in his barn at this hour, but Cade had no intention of enlightening her. He scribbled down her name and phone number on the paper, hung up with her, and then dialed the barn's bunkroom.

A ring. A second. A third and fourth. By the fifth ring, Cade started to worry that they'd had a repeat of the previous night's break-in. He slammed the phone into its cradle, snagged on a pair of jeans and his boots, then fled the room without getting a jacket. He doubted Allyson's assailant would care about his modesty.

When he got to the barn, it was locked and bore no sign of forced entry—at least not on the driveway side. He peered through the door's dusty window, but couldn't see the door on the other end of the breezeway.

Damn, maybe she was hurt. Why the hell hadn't she answered the phone?

Unlocking the door, he hurried down the

breezeway. Bailey woofed from his stall and a couple of horses poked their noses through the grain holes, expecting treats. None of the animals seemed agitated.

Cade went to the bunkroom door and pushed it open without bothering to knock.

The steady rush of the shower and a country song on the radio reached his ears. So did Ally's voice. She was singing, and beautifully.

He stopped short at the foot of her bed, surprised into a smile. A voice like that, and she worked with plants all day?

Then he looked down at himself and realized he stood half-dressed in her bedroom, while she was mere feet away in the shower. Hadn't he just been saying to himself that he ought to slow down with her?

Awk-wa-a-a-rd, sang Morgan's teenage voice in his head—something she'd said a lot while they were growing up and Cade got into blunders like this. Well, not *quite* like this.

He cleared his throat, as if she'd have heard it anyway, and turned to leave as fast as possible. As he spun on his heel toward the door, his knee banged the trunk at the foot of the bed. A loosely-wrapped parcel sitting there smashed to the floor. Muttering a swear word, Cade knelt to clean up the mess, and his knee landed with a crunch in coarse glass. Eyes watering with pain, he swore louder and shifted into a crouch. His jeans were torn and his knee began bleeding a river.

The shower, radio, and singing stopped. "Is someone there?"

"What the hell's your problem, Murphy?" he berated himself, trying to pick up the glass without getting cut again. "Get around a girl, and you're an instant dimwit."

"Hel— Oh, Cade, you scared me to death!" came

Ally's breathy voice behind him.

He turned to look, only to find her wrapped in a too-small towel, with wet hair and a whole lot of glistening skin showing.

Naked-naked-naked-naked-naked, chanted the part of him that didn't give a damn about slowing down with her. Moisture from the shower drifted across the bedroom and warmed his cool, unclothed torso, bringing with it a faint whiff of that strawberry lotion she liked so much.

With no other escape, he grinned as if they were long-lost pals who had just met on the street. "Hi."

****

Blood rushed to the surface of Ally's skin from her toes up to the top of her head. She clutched her towel closer, wishing she'd brought her robe into the bathroom after all. It lay folded on her bed on the other side of Cade. "Um...could I have...?" She forced her stare away from his broad chest and raised a hand toward the robe.

He followed her gesture with those stunning green eyes. "Sure," he said gruffly, and got to his feet.

An ugly bloodstain had spread along the torn fabric over his knee. "Oh, no! My flasks and sample jars— Are you all right?" Forgetting the robe, she stepped closer.

He turned back from the bed holding her robe, and she walked right into his arms. They bumped to a halt, chest to chest, and Ally ceased to breathe. "Cade...your knee..." she whispered.

His eyes darkened to the color of an evergreen forest at twilight. He let go of her robe and it fluttered to her feet. His hands came to rest on her hips, their heat a shock through the single layer of terry cloth separating her skin from his. The thrill of his touch blasted through her like an electric charge. He bent his head closer until his mouth hovered an inch away. "What about my knee?" he asked, his breath warming her damp skin.

She had to force the words out past the speech-stealing thunder of her heartbeat. "The glass...you're bleeding. Doesn't it hurt?"

"Yeah." His mouth brushed hers. "Want to make me forget about it?"

God, yes. She melted against him and he folded her into a solid, warm, too-tempting embrace. He slanted his lips over hers, and his tongue slipped out to trace her mouth. She gave a soft moan and threw caution to the wind. All thoughts of her work, her promotion, and her professional distance faded to insignificance.

His mouth skimmed her jaw, and then the tender, ticklish spot under her earlobe. "You drive a man crazy, Allyson. I want you so bad, I can't think straight," he whispered.

Sensual shivers raced up and down her back. He kissed a red-hot trail to her throat and she moaned again.

"I like when you make that sound," he said, pulling her closer and dragging his lips toward her collarbone.

She slid her arms around his neck and arched her head backward. Oh, sweet mercy. She thanked whatever lucky stars had made him decide to get back up and come out here.

She arched backward, confused. "Why *did* you come out here?"

"You asking me to go?" He raised his head, and disappointment flooded her at the loss of his lips on her tingling skin.

"No... That's not what— Is something wrong up at the house?" she stammered, trying to gather her fleeing thoughts.

With a sigh, he stepped back. "Your colleague called. She wants some notes or something."

"Julie? She needs them *now*?" Resentment began cooling the puddle of liquid heat that had taken up residence low in her belly.

"She seemed to think it was a matter of some urgency. Your department head wants more answers." A flash of humor lit his rugged features. "Myself, I can't see what the hurry is. I've sort of got other things on my mind at the moment." He moved back toward her.

"Urgency." Worry frosted her insides. She spun away to the little desk in the corner where she'd scattered her books and notes from the day's work.

Cade chuckled behind her. "What's the hurry, Ally? The project isn't going to get up and run out from under you in one evening."

"You don't know Julie Belhurst. I'd better call her. The number's here somewhere." She paused in her search for her notebook and looked back over her shoulder at him. "Did she *say* 'urgency'?"

His brows touched his hairline. "No, she said 'impatient,' " he replied. "Your boss, she meant. She sounded like a right pain in the ass, if you want the truth. Why are you letting her bother you?"

"Because that right pain in the ass has legs twice as long as mine, and her skirts could be headbands if they get any higher, and don't think the department boys' club hasn't noticed," she babbled as she went back to rifling the notes on the desk. God help her if Julie got that promotion. Ally would never live it down, and she'd have to kiss goodbye any hope of upgrading from her tiny, costly apartment to a real home. To say nothing of the garden she dreamed of having someday. A few sickly geraniums on a light-deprived windowsill didn't count.

Cade's body brushed up against her back and she froze where she stood. His heat radiated through the towel as he reached around her. Barely breathing, she stared at the corded muscle of his forearm.

He plucked a bright pink volume off the shelf over the desk. "This what you're looking for?"

She took the notebook and risked a look at him. He watched her, one eyebrow raised. "Thanks," she said, dropping her gaze to the messy desk.

He turned her around. With one finger, he lifted her chin so she had to look him in the eye, then he smiled. "I don't need to know Julie Belhurst," he said. "I know you, and I think you'll do fine by Hope Creek." He gave her bare shoulder a squeeze. "G'night." And he left.

Ally hugged the notebook to her chest and stared at the door long after he'd closed it. How could he be so confident in her abilities after knowing her such a short time? It'd be nice to borrow some of the sentiment.

Moreover, she wished Julie didn't have such a knack for chiseling away at her certainty in her work. She'd much rather have continued kissing Cade Murphy than spend the rest of the night poring through boring numbers and chemical equations.

"No way some miniskirt-wearing hussy is going to undermine me," she said with fresh vehemence. "She can have my data, and I hope she chokes on it." She found the phone, buried under a stack of plant pathology journals, and stabbed the numbers.

Julie didn't answer the phone—that figured— and Ally left the remaining data from the day on the machine with the return number to the bunkroom. If she had to stay up all night, she'd figure this damn thing out. Before Julie, and in spite of certain...distractions.

Even if it killed her.

Chapter Eight

Was he pushing his luck? Cade had been wondering since he woke and he still didn't have any answers. Dawn broke a mere half hour ago, and he'd already set up an army of tools, a wheelbarrow, and the water hose in the dead garden on the house's south side. The naked, thorny canes of overgrown rose bushes twisted around him. A few pathetic brown leaves clung to a hedge planted inside the plot's weathered and broken picket fence.

They'd need a whole lot of cow fertilizer if this patch of dirt was ever going to look right again. Why had he insisted on putting on this charade when he knew the problem? He tossed his leather work gloves in the wheelbarrow and studied his hand.

What the hell, why not?

Dropping to his knee—and remembering at the last second not to put weight on the injured one—he placed his palm flat on the dry, bare earth. "C'mon, honey, just one little flicker. A weed, a shoot, I don't even care what," he whispered, closing his eyes.

The wind rustled through the dead rose canes. In the near pasture, a horse whinnied to another. The faint whine of an airplane went by overhead.

Nothing else happened.

"Ah...Cade? Something wrong?"

He jumped up at the sound of Ally's voice. His flannel shirtsleeve caught in the thorns of a nearby rosebush and it latched onto him like a clutching spider. He pulled, but the thing grabbed at him as if it had a mind of its own. "Damn it."

She hurried forward to help, picking her way

with the cane over a heap of fallen fence pickets. "I'm sorry—I seem to be getting you into all sorts of trouble lately," she said, trying and failing to hide her amusement. Cade attempted to dislodge his shirt, but the leggy rose bush just kept trying to swallow him. "Here," she added. "Let me... You just..." She reached for his arm, trying to miss the thorns as he wrestled to free himself. "Hold still!" She reached again.

"Ouch!" he snarled. His arm swung forward, and then the crazy plant grabbed her, too.

Threads of her cable-knit sweater snagged in the thorns. She gave an exaggerated groan. "Now see what you did? This is obviously some cross between a rose and a giant Venus flytrap." She pulled one of the clinging canes away from his arm...only for it to snap against the front of her sweater. "Oh, for the love of— This was a gift from my parents when they went to Ireland."

"Hold on," he said. "It's about to scratch your face." He raised one arm, pulling against the thorns.

His fingertips brushed her cheek. The light touch against her skin pelted a burst of energy through his body, like a static charge without the unpleasantness.

He stilled, excitement warring with trepidation. Ally's eyes went wide, and he suspected she'd sensed the charge, too. God, if he could only tell her what he was!

Trying to master his excitement, he plucked the canes away from her sweater. "You're free, my lady," he said when he had finished.

She gave him the most adorable cocked-eyebrow smile and stepped back.

He finished extracting himself from the grasping rosebush with his heart thumping in his throat. He stole at glance at the rose cane, but it remained as naked as it had been when he'd stepped into the garden.

"Should we chop the evil critter down?" she asked. Poorly restrained laughter laced her tone. "I'm not sure I want to work in a garden with carnivorous plants in it." Her eyes shone with mirth.

Summoning a smile, which he found oddly easy while she looked at him like that, he pulled a leaf from her hair and let it fall to the ground. "We'll tame them with hedge clippers."

"We? Don't you have work to do?"

"Yep. I've got to check on the cattle out in the upper pasture—but I'll be back early this afternoon to give you a hand." He shot a look at her injured ankle.

She seemed to realize where his thoughts were headed. "I'll be safe in the garden," she promised. "I'm close to the house, and if I need help, I'll sic the rosebushes on anyone who comes to get me."

His smile wavered. He wished he could forget about their intrusions. He should have called the damn police the first time they had a break-in. He wanted nothing more than to stay by her side all day and make sure nothing else happened to her.

"Go on," she insisted, starting forward again. "You've got things to do, and I—"

As if it had read his mind, the rosebush snagged her good foot and her antique cane slipped in the dirt. She pitched forward into his arms.

Surprised into it, he wrapped his arms around her waist.

She stumbled against his body, and her thick-lashed pale-gray gaze came up to meet his. "Sorry," she squeaked.

Heat surged down each nerve ending in his body and intensified in his fingertips. In an instant, it exploded into full-blown desire to do what he'd avoided last night in the bunkroom. He swept a wayward lock of her hair away from her face, then crushed his mouth to hers.

She gave a muffled yelp, but didn't pull away. Her lips softened against his and her arms settled around his waist. She relaxed against his body, washing any possible reservations out of his head. He lost himself in her strawberry scent, in the incredible feeling of her mouth opening to his own...

And then his hands started tingling. *It is her!* He broke away, straining for a way to test that thread of power unobserved before it broke.

Ally's eyes flew open, registering confusion. "What'd I do now?"

Clenching his fists, dying to look at his hands, he said, "Nothing. It isn't you. Ally, I'm sorry, I've got to... I'll see you this afternoon." He jogged through a break in the fence, then raced around the corner of the house, out of sight of the garden. Already, the pins-and-needles sensation had begun to fade.

He dropped to one knee and slapped his palm against a weedy patch of grass beside an old water pump. "C'mon, c'mon, damn it, c'mon!"

The vanishing prickle seeped out of his fingers. He stared at the yellowed grass until his eyes watered.

And then, so gradually he might have missed it, the wilted grass began darkening. The yellow blades took on the color of dried hay, and then flushed with summer green.

Cade whooped and jumped to his feet.

Morgan's face appeared in one of the open living room windows. "What happened?"

Beaming, Cade snatched up a fistful of the grass and rushed to the window. "We're not gonna lose Hope Creek, is what." He held up the grass for Morgan's inspection.

She squinted through the window screen. Her look of puzzlement shifted to disbelief, and then surprise. "It's back? How did you do it?"

A pinprick of guilt stabbed him. He ignored it. "What does it matter? It's back. Or it's coming back!"

"Cade, that's great," Morgan said, in her typical understated way. Cade knew she was as relieved as he at the return of his gift. "Should I tell the others?" she asked.

"No, not yet. I want to make sure before I get their hopes up too much." *And get the chance to tempt Allyson into more kisses,* he thought. He shoved the looming guilt under a mental carpet.

"All right," Morgan said. Then, smiling, she disappeared from the window.

Guilt stabbed Cade a little harder. He tried shaking it off, but it clung like a burr under his skin. What did it matter if kissing her helped him get his gift back? If he got it back, the ranch would be rescued, and Ally could get her promotion, whether or not she knew how she'd earned it.

Liar, whispered his conscience. *Cheater.*

He kicked at a stone and it thwacked the water pump. Why the hell shouldn't he grab for his power if he had the chance? His family depended on it. *He* depended on it. He had every right to do what he could to provide a home for the people he cared about.

He bent once more and scattered the handful of grass on the ground. He touched his fingertips to the earth, hoping, but not expecting, his gift to flicker again. Nothing happened. He waited a bit longer, all senses alert for some remnant of that magical tingle in his hands, but still nothing came.

Dusting his hands off on his faded jeans, Kincade stood up, then stalked back toward the house. He had work to do, and plenty of it to occupy him, but he found his gaze sliding back toward the corner of the house where Ally puttered in the garden.

He smiled. She was persistent, no doubt about that.

He rounded up an extra pair of wire cutters and pliers from the top of his dresser, then left the house again. Ethan ought to be riding the fence along the north pastures by now, and Elsa would most likely be gathering eggs from the little henhouse. When he reached the barn, Cade plucked a long stem of grass from a patch beside the door and chewed its end, feeling cheerful for the first time in weeks.

When he entered the barn, he found Ally standing at the stall on the far end. Diablo's stall. She stood right beside the grill with that blasted puppy in her arms—but Diablo hadn't made a fuss. In fact, the stallion's whiskery nose poked through a gap in the grill and he was sniffing at the unusually quiet dog. Cade tensed, wondering if he ought to pull her away.

Ally's cane rested against Diablo's stall door. She shifted Bailey to one arm and pressed her other hand flat against the grill, then drew a long sigh. "We're a pair, you and I," she said. "Both of us a little intimidated, and not quite sure why we're still here."

Cade started. She hadn't seemed that way this morning or last night. In fact, she'd been downright driven since she arrived at Hope Creek. He stepped back into a wash stall, feeling like an intruder on his own property, but curiosity dug at him to find out what was wrong.

She stared through the bars at the stallion, whose hoof thumped the floor. "Well, maybe there's hope for us yet. I'll make a deal with you, boy. You start minding your manners for Cade, and I'll try to help him hang onto your home."

She turned and started back down the breezeway. Cade stepped back further into the wash stall, but his foot nudged a bucket.

She froze mid-step. "Hello?"

Damn. He abandoned his hiding place. "Want to tell me why you're hovering around that stallion when you've seen how dangerous he is?"

"He's perfectly calm right now," she pointed out.

"Yeah. How'd you manage that?"

"I came in to find a lighter shirt. It seems like it's going to get warm."

He noticed then that she had changed into a snug black T-shirt that molded to her body so well, he forgot he was supposed to be scolding her.

"Anyway," she went on, "Bailey started barking, and then Diablo seemed so curious I just stopped to see him. I think they like being roommates, after all." The pup squirmed to get down and she lowered him to the breezeway floor. Bailey scampered toward him to sniff at his boots. The pup's tail wagged like a furious metronome. "I'm sorry if I overstepped my bounds," said Ally, "but nothing happened."

"It's all right, you didn't do any harm," he said, mostly to distract himself from the way the T-shirt hugged her body.

She looked back toward the stallion. "Cade, I'm going to do my best to help you improve your land, because I don't want you to lose this place. Especially on account of me—"

Her words hit him like a dash of ice water. His earlier cheer dropped a notch. "Wait a minute," he said. "What are you so worried about? We just got started finding solutions."

Grimacing, she met his eyes once more. "I got another call from Ju—Doctor Coonan. The data I sent isn't making sense, and if I don't come up with some answers in the next couple of days, they're going to cut my field assignments."

"How can they do that? They've barely given you a chance."

"They can do whatever they want. They have to

get project funding approved by the board, and I cost money. I'm not as experienced as some of the other staff. Maybe they think they can get it done more efficiently." She spoke with nonchalance, but she rubbed her arms and turned back to Diablo.

They'd accomplished so little in the past two days. He only had a handful more to find out if she was his answer. He fought a pang of nerves and forced a grin instead. "We'll figure this out. I'll get my land in order, you'll get your promotion, and everybody's happy. All right?"

There she went again, stiffening with the air of a private facing her drill sergeant. "All right."

Hating the resignation in her posture, he jerked his chin at Diablo's stall. "Did I just hear you striking bargains with my horse, Miss Hamilton?" he asked, keeping his tone light.

She smiled then, a brilliant transformation of her features from uncertain to angelic. "I have an idea. I know you told me not to interfere with him, but I've seen my father use it with traumatized horses. I could show you this afternoon, after our work is done for the day."

"What kind of idea?"

Her smile widened. She glanced at the stallion's stall, then back to him. He felt suddenly as if he'd come out from under cloud cover and into the sun. "You'll see."

****

Ally squinted into the late afternoon glare as she sat on the paddock fence, rubbing sore muscles. She hadn't been able to tackle the entire garden herself with an injured ankle, but when Cade returned from riding fence, he helped her. Together, they turned the dry soil and worked in a bit of manure to fertilize and enrich the sad-looking rosebushes. She'd trimmed back the grasping canes and weeded almost the entire plot. Too bad she wouldn't get to see the results of her work on the roses. They might not bloom until next spring and summer.

She forced back a twinge of disappointment. Maybe Cade could send her photos. Maybe she could come see the results of her handiwork some time.

Whinnies and thumping issued from the open barn door. Cade staggered into the doorway leading Diablo, whose eyes rolled until the whites showed. The stallion's head jerked upward, halted only by Cade's grip on the lead rope. He snorted and balked. For a second, Ally feared he might pin the man against the doorframe.

"It isn't getting him outside that's the trouble," Cade grunted, wrestling with the horse's lead rope. "Getting him back *in* is the pain." He gave the lead rope a decisive jerk. The moment the stallion's head came down, he unclipped the rope. Diablo bolted into the pasture, mane and tail flying, tossing his head left and right.

"My father used to hobble a leg and tire the horse out, then get it to lie down, and he'd stroke the horse's body until it calmed. It helped with trust issues," Ally said.

"Tried that." Cade shouldered the lead rope and dusted his hands off on his jeans.

Ally watched the play of muscles in his forearms, caught herself staring, and forced her gaze away. "Oh?" she prompted, struggling to master her wayward concentration.

"Had a guy out here from Oregon who was big on horse whispering," he added. "Diablo wouldn't have it." He sauntered toward the fence, then hung the coiled lead rope over a post. "It's not people he's got a beef with, so much as buildings. Problem is, he thinks people keep bringing him into buildings just to be mean to him."

"Hmm." She stared at the stallion, who had

halted in the middle of the pasture with his inky coat glistening in the late-day sunlight. She nibbled at her lower lip. "Do you have extra pastures for the other horses?"

"Yeah."

"Good. Pasture the other horses elsewhere, preferably where he can't see them. How much time do you have on your hands for the next few days?"

"Haven't exactly got any plowing to do, seeing as I have no crops."

His dimple-flashing smirk set off a chain reaction of quivers in her belly that traveled all the way down to her toes. She tried to force the unsettling feelings down, but memories of their kisses—and the impulse to repeat them—kept her gaze riveted on his face. Did she look as transparently fascinated as she felt?

Mustering her resolve, she said, "All right. I'm going to keep working on your garden. I want you to sit here by the barn with a few apples." There. That would put him at a safe distance for a while and gain her some much-needed breathing room. Maybe then, she could control herself and concentrate on the impossible task her department had handed her. Miracle in one week. Less than that.

"That's it? Sit here with apples?" he asked. "Don't you need help in the garden?"

"Yes," she told him. "But you need to be here all day, if that's what it takes. You did most of the hard work in the garden today. All I need now is to test the control area with a few different fertilizers and get some numbers. If something works, we try more of it."

"What good is sitting on my butt all day going to do anybody?" he demanded.

She gestured toward Diablo. "It'll do *him* some good. The idea is, you're the only companion available to him tomorrow, and the next day, and the next. If he wants company and apples, he'll have to approach you...and you'll be sitting right next to his evil nemesis, the barn. Every day, try to get him a little farther inside. But *he* has to make the choice, not have it made for him."

Kincade chuckled, and the pleasant sound followed the path of her earlier quivers. "Who's the horse, and who's the owner?"

"Look," she tried again, "my dad knew a guy who rehabbed a horse from a barn collapse once, and this worked. It's worth a shot, just to show Diablo the barn won't hurt him. And people won't, either."

He smiled, and what remained of her composure began rocksliding away. Lord, what a smile he had. He did it so little that every time, it turned her insides to melted butter. Just looking at the devilish curve of those lips, a woman might be tempted to throw herself into his arms.

Except now, she didn't have the time to spare, no matter how she wanted to.

"Dinner's going to be ready in half an hour," Elsa called from the barn doorway. "Morgan just called down. And we're having company."

Cade turned his attention to Elsa, freeing Ally from that blazing green stare. "Who?"

"Sheriff MacAdam."

"Hell," Cade said, and an apprehensive shiver skipped up Ally's back. He turned his gaze on her once more. "We might not *get* to work with Diablo."

She stared across the pasture, where Diablo cropped grass, his long tail swishing. Had Paul and Maryanne called the sheriff to come and take the horse? What would happen to Hope Creek if Cade and his family lost another valuable animal? Elsa had mentioned that although Diablo's personality had soured, he still brought high stud fees because of his stellar pedigree, and many of his foals were themselves champion horses. If the sheriff took the horse, that income was as good as gone.

One more reason she couldn't afford to continue along the treacherous path of her attraction to Kincade. He needed her to focus on her job.

Even as she thought this, she found her attention drifting back toward the broad-shouldered man standing beside her. He didn't notice her stare. His own remained on the grazing stallion, and his posture had gone rigid. No doubt he was thinking the same things as she. *Some* of the same things.

Diablo, who had begun working his way closer to the fence, stood with his hindquarters angled away from them. That, more than anything, gave Ally pause. The stallion wasn't posturing as if to kick or ward off an attack. He seemed content to continue wandering the paddock in search of tasty grasses. "There isn't a mean bone in that horse's body," she said.

"Could have fooled me," rumbled Cade.

"Cade, look at him," she insisted. "If my father could see him now..." She slid off the fence. "He isn't acting like he wants to hurt anyone. We can help him."

"We won't get the chance if MacAdam decides to take him," said Cade. His mouth had thinned to a hard, grim line.

She laid a hand on his arm and found the muscles taut. "Then we don't give him the chance."

Taking advantage of the time remaining until dinner, Ally returned to her bunkroom to get the results from her work in the garden. Though her basic on-site testing kit only gave her preliminary numbers, it would help guide her efforts.

When she examined the results of the day's work, however, the puzzle only intensified. Absolutely nothing was wrong with the soil's chemical composition. The N-P-K ratios echoed the tests she'd done on other areas of the ranch. They were good even before she and Cade had worked in the garden's fertilizer—ideal, in fact, for growing the hay and silage he needed for his livestock.

His adamant opposition to chemicals precluded that as a factor in the poor growth. Weather hadn't contributed any significant problems. The only possible remaining explanation was mechanical damage. But how could the entire ranch have been affected?

"I'm missing something," she said. "Maybe I've skipped testing some important area." She thumbed through her notebook once more with a growing sense of unease. She had no time to test every square inch of Hope Creek's vast acreage.

She stuffed the notebook under her arm and left the bunkroom, leaning on her cane as she went. Her ankle had taken an unfair share of abuse today, but she hadn't wanted to leave off her work to rest it any more than necessary.

When she exited the barn, she found Ethan striding toward the house and joined him. "I'm starved," he said.

"Me, too," she agreed, and her stomach rumbled assent. "How did it go in the pasture today?"

"Ran into Brady."

"How do you 'run into' someone on such a huge ranch?" she wondered.

"I was on the property line. He was out riding with a couple of his men. Says he's been losing cows. He thinks there might be wolves or mountain lions, God only knows what, but they can't find any signs," Ethan explained. He looked up then. Following his stare, she saw a truck with a horse trailer parked beside a stylish sedan in the driveway. "Who's this?" he asked.

"The sheriff is here for dinner," said Ally. "I think he might try to impound Diablo because of the incident with Maryanne."

"Ought to impound Maryanne," Ethan said, and Ally felt a rush of kinship with him.

They arrived at the house to find not only Sheriff MacAdam, an austere man with steel-gray eyes and hair, but an older man with a crisp, wide-brimmed cowboy hat. Morgan had set an extra place at the table for him.

Cade pulled out a chair for Ally. "Hope you're hungry," he said with an easy tone she knew had to be forced. "This is Maryanne's father, Mayor Jim Sagerton."

Oh, this couldn't be good. Sheriff MacAdam sat down and accepted a plate of food from Morgan. The mayor smiled at Ally and removed his hat, hooking it over the back of his chair. "Nice to meet you," he said.

"You, too," she said, but disappointment gnawed at her. Mayor Sagerton had no doubt come to see that Cade handed over Diablo in return for his daughter's injury. She wondered if the man had come straight from the hospital.

Focus on your work, she told herself. There was nothing she could do about Diablo if the sheriff decided to take him. Cade took a seat beside her and started loading his plate with chicken and potatoes. He acted as though nothing were out of the ordinary, but she had learned enough about him to know that he had to be wondering about his next move.

Dinner passed pleasantly enough, but as Morgan presented a lemon meringue pie for dessert, Sheriff MacAdam cleared his throat. "I'll need to take a look at that stallion of yours, Cade."

Cade nodded and the hard line of his mouth reappeared. Around the table, each of his foster siblings had adopted the same grim demeanor, no doubt seeing the remainder of their livelihood sliding away.

"Give us a day or two," she said before she could

stop herself. Cade, his brother, and sisters all stared at her.

The sheriff paused with his fork halfway to his mouth. "The animal attacked someone, Miss Hamilton, and I don't recall it being your decision."

"But he's not vicious. They spooked him. Elsa, you were there. He was fine until they entered his paddock," Ally protested.

"Are you saying my daughter made that horse kick her?" demanded the mayor. He glared at her over his cup of coffee.

"He didn't mean to, I'm sure of it," she said.

"What makes you an expert in animal behavior?" asked the sheriff, clearly doubting she'd ever seen a horse at close range. "I thought you were a plant scientist."

Word spread fast in Sagerton. Complete strangers seemed to know who she was, and she'd only been in town for a few days. "I am, but my father's a vet, and he's worked with horses for most of his career. Isn't Diablo a big part of Hope Creek's financial support? Taking him could jeopardize the ranch's income. Give Cade a chance to prove he's not dangerous."

The mayor's expression darkened. "You've got until Monday, Kincade, and that's if the horse doesn't try to kick or bite anyone else when we look at him." He shoved his plate away.

Everyone stared at her, and she could almost see the wheels turning in their heads. Her cheeks grew hot and she fought the urge to sink under the table. She felt nosy and presumptuous, butting in on an issue in which she had no business.

But when she met Cade's eyes, she saw a warmth that pushed her self-conscious doubts away. His expression made her feel as if she could pull off anything.

Even a miracle.

Chapter Nine

After dinner, Cade brought Jim and the sheriff out to Diablo's paddock. The stallion showed no particular interest in them even when they entered the paddock through the barn doorway, but Cade noticed that the animal stayed as far away from them as possible. After several minutes of this, the sheriff stuffed his hat onto his head. "I've got paperwork to do," he grunted. "I'll be back on Monday afternoon."

Jim looked unhappy with that, but he followed the sheriff back into the barn.

When they had gone, Cade turned to Ally. "Thanks for putting your two cents in."

She beamed. "I thought they were going to throw something at me when I suggested they give you time to prove Diablo's not vicious. They looked like I'd asked for the impossible."

"I don't know that they're wrong on that," said Cade, scratching his head, "but at least it buys us a couple of days."

"Speaking of which," she added, "I have to make a trip tonight to the farm store in town. If I'm going to test fertilizers, I'll need a few ingredients."

"Tonight?"

"Yes. The sooner I get the soil up to snuff, the better, with only a few days on my side."

She sounded like he had when he first realized he'd lost his power. Nervous. Stressed. Desperate. All his own doubts crowded into the pit of his belly. Cade stuffed them back down where they belonged. "I can take you, if you want."

"I can find my way," she said. "But when I get back, if you'll still be up, I could use some help mixing test batches."

Chemicals. He hated to admit defeat by using them on any part of his ranch. *But what's more important?* asked the voice in his head. *Your pride, or your home?* He sighed. "All right. Just come up to the house and get me when you get back. I've got some things to do, anyway."

Cade watched her sedan leave from his bedroom window. The red glow of the taillights grew smaller and smaller as the car reached the end of the ranch's driveway, and then the lights disappeared as she drove away down the road. Even though she didn't even sleep in the house, and his brother and sisters were there, the ranch seemed a whole lot quieter without her.

Ethan had gone to bed and his sisters were in the living room watching a movie. Cade decided to go outside and test his gift again. While he was at it, he'd have plenty of time to ride up to the mountains and check on Ethan's report about the sunflowers. He might find some answers on bringing back his power. Anyway, it beat pacing his bedroom.

Why the hell had he decided to continue this insane battle with his dying gift? One week couldn't do much to improve the vegetation around here, when he'd been struggling with the problem for almost a month.

But if Ally could still find the determination given such odds, he could do no less.

He threw on his barn coat and left the house. Gravel crunched under his boots and he keyed open the barn door.

Horses nickered as he entered. Bailey gave a sleepy whine, then fell silent. He turned on the light and tacked up Dancer, an older paint gelding who was used to night rides. "What do you say, old boy?"

he murmured. The gelding snorted and nudged him as Cade slipped the bridle over his head. Cade patted the horse's neck and led him outside, where the cooling air carried the tang of pines and the earthy scent of livestock.

His favorite time to ride. No one around, no one pulling at him or needing something from him. He swung into the saddle and directed the gelding's nose toward the mountains.

For the next several minutes, the only sounds were the crickets and the thump of Dancer's hoofbeats. They passed the burbling stream and rose up into the mountains. Cade breathed in the cool air and stared at the crystalline stars overhead. Here at Hope Creek, he had breathing space from the rest of the world. He soaked up the peace like a dry sponge, letting it wash through him and fill every crevice. For the first time in weeks, he ceased to think about his problems.

The trail wasn't hard to find on such a clear, bright night. When he reached the spot where he and Ally had kissed, he found swaths of nodding sunflowers that came to his bootheels in their stirrups. Moonlight silvered their leaves and broad faces as though sealing the promise of hope. Excitement flashed through him. Here at last was proof that he could save his family's home.

He slid from Dancer's back and tied his reins to the same tree he'd used before. With his heart thudding, he bent at the edge of the swath and touched the soil.

A rustle in the field of sunflowers broke his concentration before he had the chance to test his gift. Cade rose to his feet, cautious. Several yards away on the other edge of the field, the fibrous stalks bobbed as though caught in a boat wake. He considered calling out, but decided against it. If it were an animal, it would flee regardless of his call. If a friend, they would have announced themselves. And if not a friend...

Well, Ally was safe in Sagerton by now.

He swung back up into Dancer's saddle and nudged the gelding into a trot. No point being silent. The intruder would have assumed Cade would investigate. He directed the horse into the trees, following a deer path. The old horse knew these trails and could navigate them almost as well as any wild thing that lived up here. Cade didn't worry about the animal's surefootedness.

As he rode on, the brush on either side swept his legs. He halted the horse and listened.

Something whizzed past the gelding's nose. Dancer snorted and shied backward a step. The missile thwacked into a nearby tree with the sound of a dart striking home. Twigs cracked. Leaves rustled frantically.

His night visitor was escaping.

Cade reined the gelding around in the tight space. "Get off my land!" he roared. The sound echoed in the forest canopy.

Dancer fought to turn around, backing into shrubbery and then nickering when it poked him. Cade clucked his tongue. The gelding broke into a trot back the way they'd come, following the sound of his fleeing quarry.

By the time they returned to the sunflower field, Cade lost the trail. The trespasser had taken more care to be silent now, or else had found a trail that wasn't overgrown and used it to escape.

Damn.

Cade searched for signs of a fresh trail, but the intruder had skirted the sunflower field and left no broken stalks to guide him.

Whoever it was couldn't simply have walked onto the property unless he were desperate to be there. On foot, such a journey would have taken at least an hour from the house alone. Patting the horse's neck, Cade circled the sunflower field, looking for the escapee's reason for being on his land.

Unless the reason was him.

Maybe the thing that had sped past Dancer's nose had been meant to hit him instead, and missed him in the forest shadows.

All right. This was too much. First, attacks on Allyson—twice—and now on himself. What next?

His family.

A chill raised the hairs all over his body. He jabbed the gelding's sides with his heels. The surprised horse bolted into a canter. Muscles bunching and uncoiling, he raced back down the trail to the foothills. Cade gave the animal his head, hoping Dancer didn't slip or misstep, but he couldn't afford to be careful. He swore and cursed himself for traipsing off on a night ride when he'd known someone had been lurking around the ranch.

Once again, he'd endangered his family.

Once again, his foolish impulses had led to trouble.

Only this time, the consequences might be much worse.

****

Allyson left the farm store with her arms loaded with bags of fertilizer ingredients, struggling with her cane as she went. Her eyes watered at the nose-tickling, acrid odor of the chemicals and additives. She still couldn't believe she'd managed to talk Cade into using chemicals at all. Maybe if she got favorable results, she could soften him up for a test on one of the pastures. Provided she got results quick enough.

One of the bags began slipping in her precarious grasp. She grabbed at it, hoping it didn't explode open on the sidewalk, and bumped into someone coming from the opposite direction. "Excuse me," she said.

A woman with an iron-gray bun and flour-dusted apron put a weathered hand on Ally's shoulder to steady her. She caught the slipping bag. "Can I help you, dear?"

"Oh. Thank you. My car's just over there." She gestured with her chin at her vehicle, parked down the street at the curb.

The older woman followed her gesture, then fixed her with a sharp look. "You're the new girl workin' for Kincade, ain't you?"

Remembering her run-in with the gossipy women from the general store, Ally grimaced. "Uh...yes," she blurted, unsure what to say that wouldn't set the rumor mills buzzing any more than they already were. Her cheeks flamed and she wished the streetlights would blink out.

The woman gave her an understanding smile. "I don't bite, sweetie...unlike some of the old peahens in this town." She eased another bag of fertilizer from Ally's arms. "Rose Conklin. I work at the Main Street Diner." She tipped her head, indicating a little café back down the street with checkered curtains in the windows. "How's he been doin' holding on to that pretty little piece of property?"

Something in the woman's sympathetic tone softened Ally's resolve. "Does everyone in Sagerton know what everyone else is doing?"

The woman laughed. "A city girl, huh?"

"Is it that obvious?"

"Only an outsider would wonder why we're into everyone else's affairs. We sorta take it for granted that we peek in each other's windows."

Ally stared at the woman until Rose laughed again. "I'm joshin', dearie," said Rose. She followed Ally to her sedan. Ally opened the trunk, and Rose helped her pile the fertilizers onto an assortment of jumper cables, bungee cords, and greenhouse cartons. When she turned back to the woman, she found Rose staring into the back seat of her car. Among the things littering the seat were a few glaring pink notices from her landlord that rent was overdue. Ally blushed again.

Instead of commenting on the late slips, Rose asked, "Honey, why don't you come to the diner for some pie and coffee? The locals are gone by now."

"It is sort of late..." Ally faltered, imagining her remaining research time spilling away like the contents of an hourglass.

Rose favored her with a long, kind look. "I know a kindred spirit when I see one," she added.

Disarmed, Ally agreed. Rose ushered her to the diner just in time to avoid the first plump drops of a summer rain. Ally frowned and hoped that it wouldn't continue through the night. She wanted dry conditions for testing.

Rose flipped on a single light over the diner's bar counter. She pushed through a set of swinging doors into what must have been the kitchen, then called out through a long open window to Ally, who took a seat at one of the patched-vinyl barstools. "Do you like your apple pie with or without whipped cream?"

"With," said Ally. She grinned. "Is there any other way to eat it?"

"A woman after my own heart," Rose called. She emerged from the kitchen with a pair of plates. She set them down, and moments later a couple of hot cups of coffee completed the snack. Rose sat beside her at the counter with a sigh that sounded like it came from her toes. "Ohhh, that's nice. I keep tryin' to retire and get off my feet for good. The townies keep hollerin' at me not to."

"You don't talk like you're from here," Ally said, noticing for the first time that the woman didn't have quite the same twang as the rest of the Sagerton natives. She shoved a bite of pie into her mouth, and then smiled as the complex, sweet-tart flavors burst onto her tongue. Small wonder that no one wanted the woman to quit cooking, if the rest of the diner's offerings were this good.

"I'm what you'd call a displaced Californian," explained Rose. When Ally stared at her she added, "Oh, yes. I went to cookin' school and everything. This was years ago."

"Wha-yu-hrrr?" Ally asked around her mouthful.

Rose didn't seem to mind the faux pas. "Oh, I got talked into it," she answered. "I met a young man at the school who wanted nothin' more than to show Montana what wonders it could do with a five-star chef. Handsome fella. Real, real fine. We were together ten years."

Ally swallowed her mouthful, then chased it with a gulp of perfectly-brewed fresh coffee. "What happened, if you don't mind my asking?"

"Cancer. We never married, he and I, and was that ever a source of talk." Rose sighed again, but this time she gave Ally a wry smile. "Anyway, by the time he died, I sorta fell in love with this dusty little hamlet. Now, you. You got yourself an interestin' pickle, there, in our Kincade."

The mere mention of his name sent an enticing little ripple through Ally's belly. "Wh-What do you mean?" she asked, trying for nonchalance.

"Don't tell me you've been here a handful of days now, and still managed to avoid the rumors." The older woman tapped her fork on her dessert plate and angled her head. " 'That Kincade's nothing but trouble,' " she quoted in a high, affected voice. She lowered her tone and imitated another voice. " 'I swear I saw someone pouring bleach on my garden last night, Vi, and it's just ruined. All my prize hollyhocks!' " Rose tossed a napkin on the counter.

"As if anyone cares about that busybody's garden enough to ruin it."

Vivid memories of gossip rushed Ally. Bea and Viola had spoken of a mine explosion, one Cade himself might have caused. Unable to suppress her raging desire for more information, she asked, "What did he do that makes them want to spread rumors like that?"

"Oh, Cade's been trouble since he bought Hope Creek. He's mouthy at the town hall whenever some big company wants to move into Sagerton. He figures in return for helpin' them get corporate tax breaks, we'll just get smog and extra traffic. Well, he's probably right."

Ally smiled. That went right along with what she knew of Cade. Then the looming cloud of that gossip descended again. "But I heard something about a mine—"

"Foolish people spread foolish rumors," Rose said. "Cade ain't gonna go endangerin' people by blowin' up a mine. It collapsed, all right. All them kids was hurt from it. But I've known him since he was knee-high to a grasshopper, and he doesn't have a malicious bone in his body. 'Less, o'course, someone threatens his family." She scooped up her last bite of dessert, then gathered Ally's empty plate on top of her own. "Nice pie, eh?"

"Sinful," Ally agreed, staring wistfully at the crumbs.

"My Charlie's recipe. You take the rest home to Cade and his sisters. Tell 'em hi for me."

"I will," answered Ally. She slid off her stool, then grabbed her cane and purse from the counter.

Rose wrapped up the remaining apple pie. She pressed it into Ally's hands. "Don't you listen to them talky old cranks. Cade's a good man."

"I know," responded Ally, and her heart gave an extra thump as she said it. She couldn't wait to get back to Hope Creek. She and Cade would mix up some fertilizers, and first thing in the morning she'd apply them to carefully plotted areas of the garden. Then, she'd plant a test crop. A bean, maybe. Something fast-sprouting, easy to grow. They'd fix Cade's problem, side by side. Her heart made that extra thump again, and then it gave a sad little squeeze.

One week was way too short.

Chapter Ten

Cade raced back to the house and dismounted almost as soon as he reached the porch. He left Dancer's reins dragging in the gravel, then raced up the steps and shouldered the door open.

His bootsteps echoed down the hallway and into the living room. He found Morgan staring out the back windows. Elsa had fallen asleep in the chair. When Morgan saw him, she put a finger to her lips and tilted her head toward Elsa.

"Did you see someone?" he whispered.

Morgan shook her head. "I heard a vehicle. I thought it was Ally coming back, but it came from back here, not the driveway."

He squinted out the windows, but could see nothing other than the watery silhouette of mountains in the oncoming rain. "I was followed just now, up in the mountains. That'll be the same person, or people, I bet. I'm staying up tonight. You make sure Ethan knows to keep an eye out for trouble."

She nodded. "Cade..."

"What?"

Frowning, she looked away. "Don't you think it's better to... I mean, if it's going to get dangerous... If people want us gone so badly, why stay?"

Dismay punched him in the belly. How could she ask such a thing? Hadn't they fought tooth and nail to stay together, to keep the ranch running as their sanctuary since they were old enough to live on their own? "Would you rather run from everyone for the rest of your life?" he demanded. "This is my home.

I'm not getting scared off it."

She chewed at her bottom lip, and then nodded. "All right. Then Sunday, we're going to the church picnic. Don't look at me like that. If you want to find out who's been sneaking onto the ranch, we might learn something by keeping our ears open."

He shrugged to ease the tightening of his shoulder muscles. The thought of attending a church function, with all the gossipy townsfolk whispering about them, brought back unpleasant memories of his youth. But Morgan was right. The time had come to get the jump on trouble before it slithered onto the ranch again. He vowed to make sure no one could set foot on Hope Creek without his knowledge.

Even if he had to give up sleep.

He finished putting Dancer back in his stall just as Ally returned. The barn door creaked open and she stepped into the breezeway with an armful of bags. Rainwater dampened her hair and jacket.

He went forward and took a few of the bags from her hands. "How was your drive?" he asked as calmly as possible.

"Fine. Thanks, my arms are killing me. Be careful with that one, it's a pie from Rose Conklin." She leaned on her cane for a moment. "What's the matter?"

"We had another mystery visitor," he admitted, and she stiffened. The rush of relief to see her safe surprised him. "I'm staying up, so I'll be spending the night out here with you."

He hadn't meant anything more than his intention to hang around the barn for the night, but the instant the words left his mouth, his gaze found hers. A faint blush reddened her cheeks, and his statement began to take on all sorts of interesting meanings. He noticed a fluttery pulse at the base of her throat. Her stare flicked between his eyes and his mouth.

She backed away. "I have data to set up. You—you can still help me with the test batches if you want." She sounded noncommittal, and she broke his gaze as she spoke. He practically saw the moment the wall slammed into place.

He grabbed for her hand. "What did I do now?"

When she looked at him again, her dove-gray eyes had gone soft with a pleading note. "We have so little time, Cade."

"Exactly," he said, and suddenly he saw their remaining days trickling forever away. What would happen once she went back to the university? Would his power disappear, too? Would he see her again? He caught her hands in his and found himself not wanting to let go. He rubbed his thumbs across the soft skin of her palms.

The line of her full lips hardened and she eased her hands out of his. His devil screamed at the loss of contact. "I have markers for the plots we're going to test..." she began.

"Ally."

"...and I'm basically going to adjust the ratios of..."

"Ally."

"...the different chemicals your soil might need..."

"Ally." He cupped her chin in his hand.

She froze then, wide-eyed, and he saw the glistening, fragile film of her refusal to acknowledge him, like a bubble that would burst at a breath. Her lips parted—on more excuses?

He pressed his mouth to hers, cutting them off before she could utter them. She made a quick, surprised sound, and then melted against him. The sweet softness of her lips and her strawberry scent washed away his frustrations in a flood of triumph. *This* was the Ally he wanted. To hell with all the other bullshit. When he kissed her, it ceased to exist.

But she pushed away. "We—we need to focus. We have to get this done. Cade, we can't. *I* can't."

No, cried his devil. He had to force himself not to reach for her again. But she was gone in the next moment, taking the pie from his hands and disappearing into the bunkroom as if the kiss had never happened.

How could she ignore this? He clenched his fists, digging his nails into his palms. Couldn't she see how right things were when they kissed?

Of course not. She didn't have a ranch at stake. *Selfish jerk,* he chided himself. He shoved the guilty thoughts away and gathered up the fertilizer bags with a sigh.

Minutes later, she emerged from the bunkroom with several flasks and books. "Is there a place we can mix these?"

"There's a counter next to the feed bins," he answered, even now struggling with the conflicting and frustrating impulses battling within him.

She plunked her gear onto the counter and leaned the cane against an adjacent wall, then began paging through her books. She slipped on a pair of gloves. Cade watched the way a wisp of fiery hair kept sliding forward over her shoulder, and how she kept tucking it back. The *pat-pat-pat* of raindrops on the barn roof filled the silence while he studied her. After several moments, Ally stiffened and looked up. "What?" A faint blush suffused her pale skin again. She blushed a lot. He couldn't resist it.

He reached into a drawer under the counter and found a spool of leather lace he used for fixing tack. He cut a length of it, then moved closer to her. Sliding his hands underneath her hair, he reveled in the feel of the soft skin at the base of her neck and the silken strands in his fingers.

She stilled, eyes on the counter, but her breath came faster in the silence.

He gathered up her long hair into a ponytail, looped the lace around it, then tied the loop tighter. Smoothing her ponytail down her back, he breathed in. A hint of strawberries wafted on the still air underneath the pungent scents of horse, feed, and fertilizers. His belly clenched at the sight of the creamy skin at her neck.

Reluctantly he stepped away. Keeping his tone casual took a monstrous effort. "What do you need?" he asked.

When she spoke, her voice had gone high and breathy. "That bag. The blue one, open it for me," she said. Her eyes remained on her work, but he saw her knuckles whiten as she grabbed a flask.

He could think of a million things he'd rather be doing than playing with chemicals all night. He tore open the top of the bag, then helped her measure out this powder, that granule, a quantity of water. She kept up a running commentary, building a blockade of words brick by brick. He didn't give a damn about potassium or nitrogen or soil percolation. He'd much rather have taken her in his arms again and planted a kiss on her that would make her forget all her facts and figures.

He shifted where he stood, acutely aware that a bed was mere steps away, and he and Ally would be together all night. She kept right on working. He cleared his throat. Mostly because he wondered what they'd do with the rest of the night, he asked, "How long's this gonna take?"

"Not long," she answered. "I've decided on five areas that we'll mark off and spray with different mixtures, and the remainder of the garden will be a control area where we do nothing. I bought some beans to plant..."

Damn, she was cute with all her attention fixed on those stupid jars and cylinders. He started toward her again, intending to do what, he didn't know.

She handed him two of the flasks. "Do you have a shelf where we can put these for the night? Somewhere out of the way, so they won't get broken by any of the barn cats?"

A tiny sting of indignation ran through him. Did she even notice what being near her was doing to him? "Sure," he said, and took the stoppered flasks. He pushed them onto the shelf over the counter, all the while holding her gaze.

Hell if he wouldn't make her see what they could do with the rest of the night ahead of them.

****

Without something to occupy her hands and attention, Ally's conflicted emotions zoomed up the scale to near-panic. She couldn't get involved with him, not now when her career hung by a thread. If Doctor Coonan found out about her relationship with her client—Lord, if *Julie* found out—she'd be buried in some tiny lab for the rest of her life, squinting at a computer and cranking out vegetation maps based on more important people's data.

But he stared at her with those steamy green eyes, and she forgot what was so important about their past hour of effort. His gaze meandered down her body to her worn-in sneakers. She suppressed a shiver and looked away, wishing she could take off her jacket to air her heated skin without looking too obvious.

A puddle of water lay on the floor between them, remnants of their work. She stepped toward the counter for a paper towel. "We better clean up," she said. "Someone could sl—"

Her sneaker skidded out from underneath her. Pain blazed up her leg from her injured ankle, and she toppled right into Cade's arms.

He pulled her tight against him. A not-quite-smile quirked at his lips, bringing out that sinful dimple. "You seem to keep doing this with me," he said, his voice almost a purr. "Is it intentional?"

She didn't answer. Already, the pain had dulled to near nothing. He held her attention the way a hunting lynx mesmerized its prey.

He grinned then, breaking the spell. "You were saying?"

Heat flashed through her body. Her disobedient fingers molded to the solidness of his waist under his coarse barn coat. "Sorry," she mumbled, and tried to stand upright again, but he held her still. She dared to look upward.

"Are you?" he asked. The corners of his eyes crinkled in the sexy hint of another grin. "I'm not."

Her insides twisted into a tug-of-war. His smile set off heat waves that radiated through her body to her very core. Was this the same man she had thought so distant? Dear God, how would she last out the week in his company?

His grin faded then. Ally wondered if something of her internal struggle had shown on her face. Then his gaze shifted away as though he were looking for something. "What?" she asked. "Did you hear a noise?"

He glanced at the shelf where her flasks rested, but quickly looked back to her. "Nothing," he said, and the smile returned.

Her skin sang where he brushed against her. His fingers kneaded her waist. Chills that had nothing to do with being cold sped through her body. She stared at his mouth and wished she had never kissed him. It would have been so much easier to resist him if she had never known the magic of which that mouth was capable. Her body betrayed her and arched against his.

That mesmerizing smile reappeared and he swooped down to kiss her. The tiny voice in her head pleading *no* drowned in a flood of *yes*. His tongue swept inside her mouth to dance with hers. A shudder rushed through her. Surrendering, she leaned into him.

His lips left hers only to move to her ear, where he took the sensitive lobe in his teeth. He tugged the leather lace from her hair and it spilled loose again. "I want you," he whispered.

The tickling warmth of his breath sent gooseflesh speeding over her skin. Ally sensed the hovering reasons for her not to go through with this, like specters at the edges of her vision, but she forced them to retreat. She forgot botany, forgot her ankle, forgot her own name. There was only Cade, only this very moment, where all that mattered was that he continue touching her as he did now.

His lips traveled over her throat. With a blissful sigh, she tipped her head back. His stubble scraped the tender skin, and burning need chased her shivers away. "Oh, Cade..."

His arms slipped around her until his hands cupped her buttocks. He lifted her against him. Ally curled her legs around his waist, drawing a sharp breath when his hardness pressed against her.

He groaned and backed her up to the counter. His hands roamed up under the hem of her jacket and shirt to the bare skin underneath. When he shifted away again, she whimpered a protest, but he was already slipping her jacket off her shoulders.

She tried to help him, but rather than slide the coat off her forearms, he held it there. Her hands remained caught in her sleeves behind her. "No," he said. The sound vibrated against her neck. "I want to taste you."

Another shiver sped along her nerve endings, this one sensual and delicious. He pushed her T-shirt up over her head, and that tangled in her forearms, too. A chill swept across her belly in the cooling air, only to heat again with his breath. She felt wanton, displaying her body for his pleasure. Cade dragged his tongue along her midriff and she gasped, tightening her legs around him. Closing her eyes and relishing the feel of him, she arched back and lifted her chin to allow him greater access.

That wonderful mouth traveled upward again, and then stopped above her breasts. She opened her eyes to find him staring up at her through sooty lashes almost too beautiful to belong to a man. Her heartbeat pounded. Would he stop? *No,* her body cried, and this time it was she who bent closer for a kiss.

He lifted her into his arms again. Her jacket and shirt slipped off. She didn't care where it landed. In the puddle, in a heap of dirt and spilled chemicals, it didn't matter—so long as he didn't stop kissing her. Her hair spilled forward over their faces, tickling her nose as he turned.

"Never cared about a foal watch bunk," he muttered against her lips. He lifted her higher, and then her back pressed against smooth, warm wood. She heard the old-fashioned latch click. "Didn't think we needed a bed in the barn," he added into the hollow between her breasts. She squirmed in his arms, wishing away the thin satin fabric of her bra and moaning in frustration when it didn't vanish.

The bunkroom door creaked open, then thumped shut behind them. Cade laid her on the bed. Outlined in the moonlight filtering in from the curtained window, he let his burning-hot mouth trail back down over her midriff. She arched upward, wanting him to kiss her everywhere at once. "Liking the foal watch bunk right now," he growled into the ticklish skin around her navel.

"Me, too," she gasped out. His fingers slipped over her waistband and began undoing the button of her jeans. She tried to help him remove his coat. He knelt over her, shucking it off with an impatient yank that took his shirt, too.

Liquid heat pooled in her belly. He was incredible, a sculpture of rugged masculine art carved just for her to admire. She stared from the corded muscle of his arms to well-molded pecs and down the narrowing vee of his waist. A faint line of hair arrowed downward over his lean belly. "You do work hard, don't you?" she asked, riveted to that six-pack torso.

He gave her a dizzying grin that was more devilish than humorous. "At lots of things." He bent over her once more to deliver a steaming kiss, and then his hands returned to her waistband.

Ally helped him remove her jeans. He slipped them off, cradling her injured ankle like she were made of spun glass. Her jeans puddled on the floor, and then her panties and bra followed.

His hands on her cool, exposed breasts eclipsed everything she'd hoped for. Curling her arms around him, she arched into his palms. How could she have wanted to resist this? She traced the stubbled line of his jaw with gentle nips. He gave a low growl and pressed his hips into hers.

She answered with a gasp, and then another when his mouth closed over one peaked nipple. "Mmm," he murmured against the taut skin. "You taste as good as you smell. I'm buying stock in that strawberry stuff."

"I'll get a case of it," she promised, reaching for his pants.

His hands closed over her fumbling fingers. With his smoking, grass-green eyes blazing into hers, he guided her hands until the button popped open. Her fingertips skimmed his coarse belly hairs. He groaned and pressed against her once more. She hurried to unzip his jeans, longing to feel all of him. His hands molded to her curves, branding her body with his touch as he lifted his hips to let her slide his pants off.

Able to look her fill of him at last, she found herself trembling with a desire she had never experienced. He hovered over her with a protectiveness that made her feel as treasured as rare diamonds.

His hardness pressed against her inner thighs. She inhaled sharply when his searching hand replaced it. Moisture gathered between her legs. Her skin hummed like the expectant buzz of summer insects awaiting a rainstorm.

Cade slid further onto the bed, shifting her until she lay back against the plush down pillow. His eyes roamed along her body. "I don't think I've ever seen anything so perfect," he said. His fingers inched higher.

Please, Cade. Oh, please, she begged silently, lifting her hips. Another rush of moisture joined the first.

He didn't disappoint. His fingers slipped inside her and his touch fired her senses into white-hot overdrive. She cried out as surges of ecstasy cascaded through her. Pleasure seared her again and again while he stroked her.

When she floated back down and remembered where she was, he gave an approving sort of growl and withdrew his hand to sweep it along her thigh. He nudged her knees apart. With a wicked smile, he eased downward.

The lazy afterglow of her peak disappeared in a wash of surprise. She stared at him.

A low chuckle rumbled in his throat. "You didn't think that was it, did you? We've got all night here." With his eyes on hers, he bent and pressed his lips against the hypersensitive skin of her inner thigh. He winked. "Remember, I work hard at what I do."

****

Cade dipped his head and tasted her sweetness.

Her throaty cry filled the air again. She bucked against him, once, twice, again. He felt a jolt of pure male pride, followed by a quickly stifled stab of guilt. *Forget the crops,* he ordered himself. *Forget rainfall, forget chemicals. Forget that you're dying to know whether she can bring back your power for good.* Christ, he had everything a man should want right here in his arms. Must even this be tainted by a feeling of blame?

He shoved the brooding thoughts away and concentrated on her with all of his senses—the sound of her breath, the sheen of sweat on her moonlit curves, the way her fingers tightened on his shoulders when he swept his tongue over her petal-soft skin. Damn it, he'd drown in her if he had to, just to drive away the darkness threatening to drag him under. No matter what came after, he would make this a night she wouldn't forget.

Ally gave a long sigh and her body relaxed under him. The satiny curve of her calf stroked upward along his side, at once ticklish and enticing. He slid his hand along her leg and caught it, planting a last kiss on the inside of her knee. "How are you feeling?" he murmured.

"Mmmmm," she responded. Her heavy-lidded gaze found his. Even in the dim light, he could tell her cheeks had flushed with ardor. His body resounded with eagerness at her smoky look, but he restrained himself. This wasn't about him. He wouldn't let it be about him.

But then her fingers stoked downward along his belly and found his straining manhood, almost obliterating the rest of his thoughts. He tried to arch away, to retain one last hold on his self-control, but she grasped at his shoulders and tugged. "Please come closer," she said. "I want to touch you, too." And then her hands closed around his maleness again.

With a groan, he gave in and rocked his hips against the sweet pressure of her fingers. Right now, his very soul seemed a small price to pay for the feel of her hands on him.

She stroked him with torturous, feather-light touches until he shuddered, needing more, needing to bury himself inside her. She planted kisses along his shoulder to his throat. Her legs curled around his waist. Her palms slid along his spine, beckoning, pulling him down. "Please," she whispered again.

Her blazing heat against his hardness drove him to the brink. He gave an oath and slid home.

She pulled him still closer, pressing her hips into his. "Yes," she whispered when he responded with a slow, delirious stroke. "Cade... Cade, don't stop."

He couldn't if he wanted to. Every last ounce of rational thought deserted him. He lost himself in the moment, relishing the feeling of her body. For the first time in many years, nothing mattered but right now. He thrust into her, joying in her gasp, in the way she tightened around him. Again, again, a neverending, inexorable rush of sensation that spun him still higher.

And then the world shattered.

Everything went burning green, or maybe he imagined it. Power speared through him, almost intolerable in its intensity. The sawn-wood smell of the bunkroom vanished under the earthy, cool scent of a nighttime forest. He sensed motion, change, the taking-back of old vegetation into the earth, and the springing to life of new. His body seethed with his gift until he thought his heart would burst.

Allyson arched against him once more and gasped his name. He held onto her, awestruck, and stared into her eyes while she cascaded with him over the edge. His power echoed like a far-off call and then faded. He let it go, still watching her in wonder.

At last, she melted in his arms. Her lips curled into a slow smile. "That," she said, "could be habit-forming."

He stroked her sweat-damp skin and lowered his head to plant kisses on her chin, her collarbone, the swell of her breast. He said nothing, but his mind raced. She hadn't sensed the surge of his power, then—though he couldn't imagine how she'd missed it. The force had blown through him with all the supernatural noise of an earthquake in his ears.

He allowed his gaze to rove along her moonlit body to her silken hair. Letting a lock slide through his fingers, he smiled...but he couldn't look her in the eye now, and his smile came with an effort.

Here was his proof. Making love to her could bring his power back. Making love to her even more might get it to stay.

Bastard, he snarled at himself. He gave her a last kiss, wanting more than anything to languish in bed with her the rest of the night. Nothing he did now could absolve him of the feeling of having used her, but he could leave before he made things worse. "I'm sorry," he whispered, and he meant it with every cell and synapse. "I'd better go check the premises."

"I'll come with you," she offered.

He pressed her down with a gentle hand and added, "No. Rest. Your ankle needs to heal. I'll take care of things tonight."

He pulled on his pants, grabbed his shirt and coat, and then left the bunkroom with a host of demons chasing him.

Chapter Eleven

Allyson woke to the homey sounds of birdsong and whickering horses. She smiled and stretched out underneath the snug blankets, relishing the coziness.

After a few minutes, she swung her legs over the side of the bed, then tested her weight on the injured ankle. Even that seemed to have faded to a twinge. She stood gingerly. When her ankle didn't protest, she walked across the braided rug to the shower, eager to start the day and her project.

Her cheer lasted through the shower and a cane-assisted, awkward but steady walk to the main house. Last night's rain had soaked into the soil. Only the low spots bore testimony to its occurrence, with small puddles that attracted a few bathing birds who scattered as she approached. Cade was nowhere to be seen, so she assumed he must be finishing up some morning chores. Her heart skipped at the thought of him, and then pounded with the memory of last night.

She even found a buoyant smile for Elsa, when the young woman announced a fax had arrived from Julie over Hope Creek's business line. Elsa put the document into her hand, then left the kitchen to work with the cattle.

Ally scanned the fax over a bowl of corn flakes and fresh blueberries. The top of the document bore Julie's usual self-indulgent blather, and a few veiled barbs indicating that the woman was managing affairs in the department much better without Ally's presence. Ally allowed herself a spiteful moment of curiosity about what sort of "affairs" Julie might be managing. But even the department soap opera didn't bother her this morning. She skimmed the fax and found herself thinking more about Cade's strong, warm hands than Julie's machinations.

Then her eyes slammed to a halt toward the bottom of the letter. *Doctor Coonan has agreed that I should come to Hope Creek and take a progress report on your work,* it read. *He has several other proposals to review, and we've decided that because of his time constraints, I will take over supervision of this assignment.*

Fury boiled up inside Ally until she almost crushed the fax in her hand. *We* decided! Supervision! As if Julie already counted herself among the department heads and their decision-making policies. More likely, Coonan had caved to Julie's incessant nagging—or the woman's doe-eyed looks had suckered him, too—and he'd given her a supporting job at Hope Creek to pacify her. Now the woman would be breathing down Ally's neck at every turn, waiting like a vulture for her to trip up.

A bubble burst inside Ally's chest. There went any hope of being in Cade's arms again. Julie would demean it into a nasty little scandal, and then get Ally fired.

But it's not a scandal, she cried silently. *It was wonderful and romantic, and everything I could have dreamed, only better.*

The corn flakes took on the dry, stale flavor of cardboard, and the blueberries' sweetness developed an unpleasant tart undertone. Ally set down her spoon and washed her last mouthful of cereal down with a glass of milk.

Well, if Julie wanted a fight, a fight she would get. Ally would show her the best damn fieldwork anyone had ever done. She set her bowl and glass in the sink, then hobbled back outside toward the barn.

Diablo stood in the near pasture, tail swishing as he grazed. She scanned the property. There was Cade, just like she'd asked him, sitting beside the barn with a bucket of what looked like apples. He sat chewing one of them and leaning back in the chair with his legs propped against a water pump near the barn's loading door. Her heart gave a leap. "Good morning," she called.

"Morning," he responded. "Sleep okay?"

"Wonderfully," she admitted, though she couldn't help wishing he had come back to bed after all. He hadn't returned to the bunkroom since he left to prowl the barn.

His gaze flicked back toward the stallion in the pasture. "Damned horse hasn't even come close to the barn yet, and I've been out here since dawn. How long do I have to sit here and wait for him to get interested?"

Frost laced the edges of his tone. She took a closer look at him. He kept his gaze on Diablo, but she noticed a curious tension in his posture that hadn't been there last night. "I don't know," she answered. "I suppose that depends on Diablo's state of mind and your patience."

Cade looked back at her then, though only for a moment. He opened his mouth, hesitated, and then asked, "Going to start on your project? I already put the flasks out in the garden."

Suspecting that wasn't what he'd been about to say originally, she struggled with disappointment. After last night, why would he act so casual? *How* could he? She chewed her lip, wanting to talk to him about it but fearing she'd only sound clingy. Her earlier euphoric mood lost most of its warmth. "Thanks," she managed. She turned away and started toward the garden with no further comments. She didn't trust herself to say anything else.

Determined not to let Cade's mood sour her own, she plunged herself into her work. She had soaked the bean seeds overnight to speed germination. Now, she sowed each plotted patch with the same care she would have used back at the university lab. When she finished that, she spread one flask of fertilizer on each plot. Within the next few days, she hoped to see promising results.

She weeded the rest of the garden well into late morning, when a tickle at the back of her neck brought her out of her deep concentration. She looked up, but no one was around. Rising to her feet, she brushed off her dusty pants. Cade had left Diablo's pasture. His siblings were likewise absent, probably still working with the cattle or surveying the property. She did notice a shiny truck parked beside the barn. She reached for her cane and, leaning on it, pivoted in a slow circle.

She yelped when she saw a man standing on the other side of the weathered picket fence. "Hello," he greeted, staring at her from underneath the brim of his pristine cowboy hat.

She recognized Maryanne's father Jim and relaxed. "Sorry. I didn't realize you were there."

"No, ma'am. It's my fault, startling you." He gave her a broad smile and held out his hand. "I think we got off to a bad start, last time we met."

She went closer and shook his hand. "Did you need to talk to Kincade?"

"No, actually. To you," he said, surprising her. He scanned the garden, then angled his head and studied her. "I like to know who's passing through my town. Thought we could chat a bit."

His use of the words *passing through* touched a nerve deep within her. He spoke as if he thought she'd come and go without so much as a whisper to testify that she'd ever been there. She gathered up her empty flasks and garden tools and put them in the wheeled cart Cade had left for her, then reminded herself to be on her best behavior. Diablo's fate might depend on how well she watched her tongue with the mayor. "What can I do for you, Mayor Sagerton?"

"I hear you're looking to help Cade out with his troubles here at Hope Creek. That's awful kind of you, taking this on without any other people to work with you."

"I have help," she said. "I've got—" She couldn't bring herself to say *a supervisor*. "—someone coming to look in on the project."

"Do you, now? That's real good." She started toward the sagging picket gate. Jim opened it for her. When she emerged from the garden, he closed the gate, then took off his hat. "Miss Hamilton, I hope you don't think I'm being unfair to Kincade. Maryanne's my baby girl, and I can't help it if I worry for her. I'm still her pa, no matter how old she gets. I don't like to see her get hurt."

Ally felt a twinge of empathy. Thinking of her father, she smiled. "I understand, Mayor."

"Jim."

"Jim," she echoed. "But Diablo's not a lost cause. I swear to you, that horse is not mean by nature."

He cracked that broad smile again. "I have to say, I can't work you out, Miss Hamilton. Do you work with plants or animals?"

"I'm a botanist by trade, but my father's a vet, so I've picked a few things up," she admitted. "We're an outdoorsy sort of family."

"Yeah, my granddad was a big one for hunting and fishing," Jim said, angling the brim of his hat to ward off the bright sunlight. "Around here, you didn't have much choice back then. You didn't hunt, sometimes you didn't eat." He offered his arm.

Ally shook her head.

The big man shrugged and followed her toward

the horse barn, adding, "I'd sure like to see what you've cooked up to help Kincade. He says you're doing a fine job helping him out."

She paused at that. When had Cade had the chance to praise her work to Jim? A tiny spot of warmth and pride swelled in her chest. Once more, she scanned the barn's nearest pasture, but Cade still hadn't appeared.

Although, she noticed, Diablo wasn't visible either. Had the two made amends at last? Smiling, she hobbled toward the barn.

"Are you sure you don't want some help, Miss Hamilton?" Jim asked behind her.

"I'm all right," she assured him, "but if you want to come along, maybe you'll see Cade working with Diablo right now."

They passed through the barn and she entered the paddock by way of the open loading door. Jim hung back behind her. From the corner of her eye, she noticed the stiff angles of his body and the watchful way his gaze shifted around the barn and pasture. Either Mayor Sagerton loved his daughter fiercely enough to hate the horse on principle, or he was preparing for something he might not want to see. What did he expect, that the stallion would rush them the moment he noticed them?

They made their way along the length of the barn and around its back end. There, at the corner, Ally halted with an indrawn breath of pleasure and wonder.

Diablo was eating from Cade's hand.

"Well done, Kincade," Jim said. The mayor's voice shattered the still air like a thunderclap.

Diablo's head snapped up. He half-reared, almost kicking Cade, who jumped out of the way. The stallion bolted away into the pasture, swinging his head as though shaking off flies.

"Well, I *did* have him," Cade growled. He

dropped the slice of apple that remained in his palm.

"Sorry about that," added Jim. The big man came forward, adjusting the angle of his hat, and stared after the retreating stallion. "He is a fine piece of horseflesh, Cade. I hate to have the police take him in, but an animal that flighty can't be trusted. What if Maryanne had been seriously hurt?"

A flicker of guilt crossed Cade's features. His jaw muscles rippled, but he said nothing. His gaze remained on Diablo, who slowed to a stop in the center of the pasture, and then lowered his muzzle to snuff at the grass. Finally he looked away from the horse, but his gaze landed on Ally instead, unreadable. "Like to chat with you, Jim, but Miss Hamilton and I have work to do here. We'll be at the church potluck, though."

"Of course, of course," Jim answered. If he seemed put off by Cade's lack of welcome, he didn't show it. "You come sit with the Sagertons after service, and we'll talk then." He put out a big hand.

Cade shook it, and then Jim left. Only when the mayor had gone did Cade's expression change. Ally recognized the hard line of worry that firmed his lips. "With Rumble and Smoky hurt, I'm down to only a few horses if they take Diablo. I can't work cattle like this. I'll have to hire out to Brady...or sell."

She blinked. Cade had never shared his concerns so openly before. She began to think she'd judged him wrong this morning, but as soon as he made that confession, his features cleared once more into his usual stoic air. "You seemed to be doing fine with Diablo until just now," she pointed out, wanting to ease his mind.

"Yeah, real fine. Took me all morning." The bare hint of amusement in his eyes brought a pleasant flush to her cheeks and set her heartbeat thumping faster. "How'd your gardening go?"

"Good," she said. "I planted the bean seeds. I'd like to shore up that fence, though. Would you come with me and take a look at it?"

"Sure. I'm getting sick of horse-sitting anyway, and I think Diablo is, too." He picked up the apple bucket and offered her his arm.

She found she was much more willing to accept his help than Mayor Sagerton's. He curled his fingers around her arm, supporting her. The warmth of his hand on her skin brought on a delirious rush of flutters, reminding her of his skillful caresses last night. Her cheeks burned and she felt like a shy teenager with her first love.

Love. Whoa, Nellie. Ally bit her lip. Maybe that wasn't the right word for this. She wasn't ready for that to be the right word for this. *Making* love and being *in* love were two very different things. *Just you remember that,* she scolded herself.

They walked through the barn and out across the driveway, back to the garden. All the while, she wrestled with a sticky spiderweb of confusing feelings. She had no attention to spare for her surroundings until Cade swore out loud. Alarmed, she looked up.

Through the lopsided, worn picket fence of the garden, she saw a splash of vibrant green. Startled, she hobbled closer on her cane, hardly noticing the way Cade hung back.

Every one of the fresh-turned plots she'd prepared and seeded that morning now flourished with bean plants three feet tall.

****

Cade stared at the plants, his skin crawling with all the discomfort of a naked man who has found himself trapped in a crowded room. If Ally just looked, she'd see the truth blazing on him like a helicopter searchlight. He hunched his shoulders. Even his barn coat hung heavy on his frame. Any minute now, she'd turn to him and the questions he couldn't answer would begin.

She dropped her cane in the dirt and limped toward the fence. He started forward to help her, but she was already pushing through a gap between the pickets. She knelt and took one of the fibrous beanstalks in her hand to examine its leaves. Her gaze went to the soil, but no footprints besides her own showed in the earth, as he knew they wouldn't.

When she labored to her feet again, she rounded on him with eyes gone cold as iron. "I'd like to know whose joke this is. First sunflowers, and now this!"

"Ally, which of us would have wanted, or had time, to pull a joke on you?" he asked, sure that he was leading her down the path right to the truth. "You just got done planting, and you saw where I've been all day. Everyone else is working cattle or in the house."

She limped back toward him, ignoring her cane, and he had to force himself not to look away. "Then what is going on?" she demanded. "No lies, Kincade. Not after—not now." She held his gaze, but he saw by the frowning twitch of her mouth that it took an effort. She was hurt, deceived. And no wonder, after what they'd done last night. They could be honest with their bodies, but not with their words. At least he couldn't.

He steeled himself, trying to decide how best to walk the line. Part of him, a surprising and troubling part, wanted simply to throw caution away and tell her the truth. He'd never been willing to share that secret, even with Maryanne. His ex knew only the rumors.

Part of him wanted to lie through his teeth, to tell Allyson any story he could fabricate to protect his family and home. That part, he recognized. He seized it. "I thought you planted seeds."

"You think *I* did this?" Her voice rang with

indignation. "I came here to work, not to play games."

"I didn't say you were playing—"

"Well, *someone* is!" she spat. "None of my research has found the remotest imbalance in your soil. There are no insects eating up your crops. Fertilizers make no difference in growth. It's not a problem with water percolation, and it's not a lack of irrigation. It's not drought. There is no ice or snow damage, because it's the middle of flipping summer, and so my only possible finding, Cade Murphy, is that it's *you*."

A chill sputtered down his back. He opened his mouth to toss out a bold-faced lie and found it impossible. "I didn't plant those," he said instead. His words dropped flat on the ground between them.

"Who did?"

Walk away, he thought. *Just stop talking and walk away.* But he couldn't.

Without another comment, she turned and hobbled toward her car, supported by her cane. "Where are you going?" he called when she opened the car door.

"To town," she said, all meaning and inflection drained from the words. *Like a stone that can speak,* he thought grimly. She said nothing more as she started the engine, turned the old sedan around, and then rattled off down the driveway.

Son of a bitch.

He glared at the damning evidence in the garden. He should have been ecstatic about the return of his power. He should have rushed right in there to test his gift on some other piece of vegetation. But all he could think about, staring after the cloud of dust retreating down his driveway, was the accusing look in Ally's eyes.

A voice called to him from the direction of the house. He turned to find Morgan walking toward him, carrying a basket. She wore the unmistakable frown of impending bad news. "At least let me fill my belly first," he said when she had reached him.

She offered the basket, which contained three generous ham sandwiches, cookies, and bottles of lemonade. As if on cue, Ethan emerged from the cow barn and started toward them. "Where's Ally?" Morgan asked.

"She stepped out," Cade said.

They sat on a pair of upright logs beside a woodpile Ethan had stacked near the house. "She's been busy," Morgan pointed out, surveying the garden with its rambling bean plants.

"*I've* been busy," he corrected. "She didn't do that. My power did."

Morgan's face brightened for a moment, and he braced himself for a round of excitement and praise he didn't deserve. He already felt like the lowest rat in a city sewer. But his foster sister's expression vanished into concern. "Does she know?"

"She realizes something's going on. She just planted those this morning," he explained, waving a hand at the plants in the garden. "From seeds."

Ethan reached them, then pulled up another log to sit. He poked in the basket and retrieved his own lunch.

Morgan frowned. "What did you do, Cade? Why are those plants so tall, so suddenly?"

"She thinks I played a trick on her," he forced out.

"I know you didn't. What happened?"

Ethan looked up now at the warning in Morgan's tone. His gaze went from Cade to the garden and back. "Did you grow those?"

"Yes." Cade hunched his shoulders under the barn coat again.

"Hot damn. We're back in business." Ethan took a huge bite of his sandwich. He grinned around it,

149

chewed, and then stopped. His brow furrowed. "We're *not* in business."

"I didn't control it," said Cade. He itched to be away, riding fence or cleaning stalls, anything but sitting there under the sweating-hot spotlight of his siblings' attention.

"Well, what *did* you do?" Ethan asked around his mouthful. The curiosity in his studious, cat-gold eyes turned to realization, and then amusement. "You *did*, didn't you? Hell, if that's all it takes to keep this place up, why don't we just get you la—"

"Shut your yap!" Cade snarled. His voice boomed across the yard. Ethan's teeth met with a click and he rocked backward on his makeshift seat.

"Ethan, go see if Elsa needs help getting the laundry out," Morgan said.

"She's big enough to do it herself," snapped their brother.

"Ethan, please," Morgan said. "Take the basket. Ally's not here to eat her share."

He hesitated, then scooped up the basket, cussing all the way back to the house.

When he had gone, Cade felt Morgan turn the full weight of her knowing, silent stare on him. Finally, she said, "Are you falling in love with her?"

The question came so unexpectedly that for a moment he wasn't sure he'd heard right. He turned the notion away as soon as he'd absorbed it. A man in love wouldn't use the object of his interest the way he had. "It just happened," he said, shoving one of the cookies into his mouth. "Don't read any more into it than that."

If Morgan had anything else on her mind, she didn't share it, but he felt her appraisal for several long minutes. At last, unable to tolerate it any more, he said, "Didn't you have something to say when you came out here?"

"Brady called. He wanted to sell you his tractor.

The new one."

Cade paused with another cookie halfway to his mouth. "Why would he think I have enough money to buy a brand-new tractor from him? He knows we're hard put to keep Hope Creek running."

"He's lost more cows," she said. "Something up there's taking them two and three at a time and leaving no traces. He asked if we were losing any cattle."

"Not so far, but our herd's been small enough to keep a closer watch on them all. Brady's got twice the number and they're pastured farther up than ours." He bit into the cookie, then added, "Is he sure they aren't just wandering off into the mountains?"

"He didn't say, but he was pretty steamed. Some of them were the new ones he'd just bought. Do you think we should move our stock out of the summer pasture?"

"We can't buy feed and we can't afford to graze them down here. They'd starve," Cade muttered, lashing himself with the words. "Ethan will have to watch them up there for the next couple of days, and then I'll take over." As soon as he finished with Diablo, he thought. As soon as he did a million other things. As soon as he apologized to Ally.

How would he apologize when he couldn't explain how he *wasn't* tricking her?

"That's not all," Morgan added.

"What now?" he asked, cracking open the bottle of lemonade.

"I saw a fax from the college," admitted Morgan. "Ally's co-worker's coming to supervise her."

"What, her boss?"

"No, not Doctor Coonan... Her name's Julie."

Indignation lanced through his belly. Not long ago, he'd have welcomed a fresh pair of eyes to help him find a solution to Hope Creek's problems. But he knew how much Ally wanted to prove her mettle, and Julie was Ally's number one competition.

Suddenly he wanted more than anything to see Ally succeed. By hook or by crook, she'd get that damn promotion. He'd see to it.

She deserved it, after what he'd done.

Chapter Twelve

"I can't figure him out, Rose. I thought we were getting along so well." Ally hunched over the café counter as she spoke, trying to hide the blush she felt creeping into her face. "None of my research has gotten me any closer to a solution, and I can't help feeling there's something Cade won't tell me. Something that, if he just *said* it, could help me clear up whatever Hope Creek's problem is."

"I hope you're not listenin' to all that gossip after all, sweetie," said Rose as she topped off Ally's fountain soda.

"I don't even *know* the gossip."

"Listen, honey. All you need to know is, none of them has ever done the Sagerton people a bit o' harm," said Rose. She plunked Ally's soda glass back on its napkin and pushed it across the counter.

A large figure lowered itself to the barstool beside Ally. She recognized Kincade's neighbor. "Hello, Mister Hart."

"Howdy. Miss Hamilton, is it? Coffee, Rose, and a hamburger and chips," said Brady. Rose nodded and left to take care of his order.

"Ethan said you lost some cattle," Ally said.

"Yep. Hope Creek lose any?" The man fixed her with his shrewd stare.

"I couldn't tell you," she admitted. "I've been busy with my work there. No one's mentioned it though."

Brady sank into silence until Rose brought his meal, and then he was more occupied with lunch than conversation. Ally contented herself with a look around the diner. There were few patrons at this hour. Most had finished their midday lunch and gone back to work, or wherever the rest of their days took them. In a corner booth she noticed Maryanne shutting her cell phone, then stuffing it into her purse.

Ally began to slide off her barstool, but she hesitated. She burned with curiosity about Cade's ex-girlfriend, though she hated to admit it. Maryanne wore an exquisite designer blouse, slacks, and dress boots with just the right amount of casual chic. She seemed light years away from Ally's jeans-and-T-shirt slice of the world.

But in spite of all the stylish class Maryanne possessed, Cade Murphy wasn't with her now.

He isn't with you, either, reminded her inner voice. *You two had a moment and nothing more. Be an adult and get on with your life.*

Even so, she found herself marching across the café, leaning on her cane as she went. "How is your arm?" she asked.

The woman lifted her head. Her glossy curls bounced around her perfect face. "Hello. Better, thank you."

Ally couldn't resist the tiny note of accusation that slipped into her voice as she said, "You know Cade's horse still might get impounded."

Whatever Maryanne thought of Ally's boldness, she merely angled her head. "Why don't you sit? Paul won't be here for a little while yet."

Ally sat on the cushioned vinyl seat on the table's other side.

The woman watched her with an expression at least as shrewd as Brady's, but with much more personal interest. "How's your work coming at Hope Creek?"

"Fine," Ally lied, wishing she had something more impressive to tell.

"Kincade's a hardworking man. He loves that ranch," Maryanne pointed out.

Nodding, Ally said nothing.

The other woman's expression softened. "He's something, all right." The look disappeared as quickly as it had come, as if she realized she was giving away some secret vulnerability. Did she miss Kincade after all? "How long will you be staying?" Maryanne added.

"Another few days. I've gathered almost all the data possible. Now, it's just a question of processing it." *And finding the cause of those plants that seemed to grow mysteriously where everything else failed,* she added privately.

"I hope you find his problem," said Maryanne. "I'd hate to see him have to sell Hope Creek."

Stubbornness streaked through Ally. "He won't," she promised. "I'll find the problem."

"That might not be as easy as you think," Maryanne replied.

Ally felt the same irresistible pinch of suspicious curiosity she'd experienced when Bea and Viola were discussing the mine explosion. At last, someone might explain what was going on around here! "What do you mean?" she asked, trying to still the fidgeting of her feet under the table.

Maryanne paused to apply a coat of gloss to her full red lips. "By now, you must have heard the stories about Cade and his family." She favored Ally with a calculating stare. "You *have* heard them, haven't you?"

"The mine? It's just gossip," said Ally.

"Not all of it." Maryanne leaned closer. "I'm only telling you so you know why the town thinks of Hope Creek the way it does. Cade and his brother and sisters really were playing in an old mine when it exploded."

Ally felt the blood drain from her face. "How did

they survive?"

"I don't know. But none of them has been the same since. They're...different. Even the ranch is different." The woman leaned further over the table and lowered her voice. "People say Hope Creek's got the most fertile land for miles around, and *some* people say it's because of Kincade himself. They think he made a deal with the devil, because even in a drought, that ranch has grown some of the best crops and livestock that have ever come out of Montana."

Until recently, Ally corrected mentally. *What changed?* "But what caused the explosion?" she asked.

"Chemicals. Or at least that's what the fire marshal said when they investigated."

That explained Cade's resistance to her suggestion of using chemicals on his property, Ally thought.

"The kids were all checked by doctors and found healthy, and all that," Maryanne went on. "But not one of them has ever confided in the town what actually happened that day. It's always the same story, no matter which of them you ask: they don't know."

"But he must have told you." Ally had to swallow a nagging nip of jealousy. "You dated him."

"Cade's got a knack for growing things, and that's all he's ever been interested in," said Maryanne, her voice cooler now, more impatient. She seemed to want to turn the talk away from herself, or at least away from unpleasant memories. Ally wondered if she'd pried too far, but she couldn't resist leaning forward to hear the rest of the woman's explanation. "Like some people can play the stock market," Maryanne added, "or some people paint works of art...he grows things. He's been like that ever since I met him."

Laughter bubbled up from the pit of Ally's belly. "What, like magic?"

"Darling," interrupted a man, "I'm sorry I'm late. The office called from Helena. Urgent." Paul Riegel slid into the booth beside Maryanne and gave her a brief kiss on the cheek. "Miss Hamilton. Nice to see you again."

"Hello," said Ally, fully aware that the last time they'd met, Paul had been ready to have Diablo put down. She wanted, with a sudden rush of righteous anger, to show Paul how far Diablo had come in just one day. Even now, Cade must be back in that pasture coaxing the stallion to come to him with gentle words and touches.

Her thoughts took a sharper and far more intimate turn, but Paul broke in. "Will you be joining us for lunch?" he asked her.

"No, thanks," she said. "I've eaten. In fact, I have to get back to the ranch and finish work." She stood up, flustered. "Goodbye. 'Bye, Maryanne."

Ally returned to her car with as many questions about Cade as she'd had that morning. Maryanne's words only compounded the confusion surrounding Hope Creek's residents—and one stoic, green-eyed mystery in particular.

She had plenty of time on the drive back to the ranch to contemplate Maryanne's meaning about Cade's plant-growing abilities. Did the woman really think he possessed some supernatural green thumb? How absurd!

But she couldn't help thinking about those tall, lush plants in the garden, with their bean pods almost ready for picking. Impossible. She was a woman of science. If a thing couldn't be smelled, seen, heard, tasted, touched, or measured, it simply didn't happen.

She had never ended a project without discovering the problem with and solution for a client's property. But she had to admit this time she might have met a dead end.

She only hoped that Julie would come to that same conclusion.

****

"Morgan, give me a hand here with the water," Cade said. He sounded cross.

"What do you want done?" she asked, peering over the rickety fence into the garden.

Cade knelt in a patch of soil beside the bean plants with his bare fingers dug into the earth. "The soil here is still dry even after last night's rain," he said. "See if you can draw some water up into the plants. They're drier than I'd like."

"You can't force them to take on any more water than they're ready to," she reminded him.

"I know that," he said through his teeth, "but this isn't a natural wilt. My power's not at a hundred percent. These grew too fast for the water uptake to catch up with them. Since we have them, we ought to take care of them, right?" His voice grew harder. "They may be the last green things we get on this damn ranch."

Morgan stepped through the tumbledown fence and touched the nearest plant. Liquid warmth formed in her fingertips, intensified, and then stretched out through the plant's vascular system, down along the molecules of water that connected to each other.

She sensed water moving upward through the vegetation. She pulled on that movement and drew liquid into the plant's roots, slowly so as not to overload it and dilute its vital nutrients. Pressure increased along the vascular system, resistance to her gift, telling her how much and how fast she could encourage the plant to take water. When tension had reached a reasonable point, she noticed the wilting leaves stood more upright. She let go of that plant and moved to the next to repeat the process.

"Cade," she said, "what are you going to do about Allyson? You can't keep her around just to..." She paused, searching for a more delicate way to say what she wanted.

His head came up and he stared at her with a hard directness that he never gave to Ethan or Elsa. "I don't mean to. I'm not touching her again." Self-reproach seared each word.

"I know you didn't do it to use her," Morgan said, more gently. He didn't respond, so she added, "I only meant, what are you going to do now? Can you repair your power? Is it still there?"

"Enough to notice. Not enough to fix all that," he answered, jerking his chin at the vast, straw-colored acreage stretching away past the horse barn. His expression darkened again. Morgan knew he blamed himself for the ranch's troubles. He always took on much more responsibility than he deserved, from the time they met in foster care. Sometimes she wondered if he'd ever been allowed a childhood or if he'd always been old beyond his years.

"What about fixing just this?" she asked, nodding at the skeletal pruned rosebushes.

"What about it?"

"It's a start," she suggested.

With a sigh, he knelt beside a row of the bare rosebushes. The canes had been cut back from their former wildness, but the ones twining along the picket fence still remained. He gripped the end of the nearest cane in a place free of thorns and gave it that intense stare he used when calling on his gift.

Nothing happened.

"Allyson's dedicated," Morgan murmured, noting the neatly cleared plots where the bean plants grew. Her gaze traveled around the rest of the little garden, taking stock of the tamed hedges, raked earth, and pruned foliage. "She cares about this place."

"Yep," Cade said, his attention still fixed on the rosebush. His intensity softened a bit. "I half expected her to fight Jim and the sheriff single-handed when they came after Diablo."

Chuckling, Morgan finished drawing water for the remaining bean plant. "She's something. I heard she got her job by camping outside Doctor Coonan's office for two weeks."

Cade looked up. "When did you hear that?"

Morgan released the last bean plant with a laugh. "We don't all live here in a vacuum, Cade. I have friends in Bozeman."

Amusement flashed through his eyes for a moment, followed by a gleam of curiosity. "What'd she do?"

"Apparently, Doctor Coonan was interviewing for the job and she wouldn't let him tell her no. For two weeks, she bugged him to let her take on every two-bit, thankless task in the department, just so she could show him she was up to it. The rest of the staff even started asking him to give her a name badge and be done with it."

"Sounds like the Ally I know," Cade said, and the amusement returned.

Strolling around the tidied garden, Morgan touched a clipped buckthorn hedge. It needed a little water, too. She pulled some up through the root system. "I can't wait to see how she handles the raised eyebrows at the Sunday picnic. I bet they think we dragged her into some creepy science experiment."

"Or that she's running the whole show," added Cade. He cracked a smile. "Do you know she made me sit the whole day in the barnyard with that maniac stallion just to see if he'd come up to me?"

"Did it work?"

A deep chuckle rolled up out of Cade's chest. "Damned if it didn't. Until Jim showed up and scared him off, I thought I'd even get a bridle on him without a fight." His gaze turned to the pasture beside the barn.

"Jim was here?"

"Yep. Must be to peek in on our progress," he said.

"Cade, look." She touched the rose cane, which was now studded with tiny green buds. Not the explosion of the bean plants behind them, but a start. She sobered. "Then your power's return really is Allyson's doing."

"Yeah," he said, softer now. He let go of the cane and it sprang back. "The question is, why?"

"Try something else. Quickly," Morgan urged him. She gestured to a reedy patch of daisies that bore few blooms.

He plunged his fingers into the soil beside the daisies and waited. For a breathless eternity it seemed as though nothing would happen, but at last she saw the pale, yellowing stems flush with green. "The hedge! Do the hedge," she prompted.

Morgan made him circuit the entire garden, and though the results varied, his power seemed more consistent than it had been in weeks. Finally, when he'd released the last plant and she finished drawing water for it, she stepped back to survey their work.

Buds erupted along branches and stalks that had remained bare for months. A few flowers had regained their summer glory. A little patch of forget-me-nots grew beside the garden gate. Overall, the garden bore a promising freshness beyond anything Morgan had hoped. Would this burst of life and color be enough to convince Cade that his power hadn't deserted him? More likely, she realized as she watched his sober face, he attributed this to his relationship with Ally—one he'd already sworn to end.

Ally.

"Oh, Cade," she said with sudden horror, "what will she say when she comes back and sees all this?"

The crunch of gravel brought their attention to the driveway. As though summoned, Allyson had returned in her sedan. "What are you going to tell her?" Morgan whispered, though Allyson couldn't possibly have heard.

"Don't know," he replied, watching the sedan roll to a stop in Ally's parking spot. Morgan, who had always known him better than Ethan or Elsa, saw underneath his calm exterior. He wore the grim look of a man facing the gallows and racking his brain for a way out.

Allyson emerged from her car and came toward them, leaning on her cane. Her gaze landed on the garden and went dark with suspicion. Morgan forced herself to remain still. Ally's brows lifted. "Care to explain?"

Dark humor flickered in Cade's eyes, then vanished again. When he spoke his voice was calm, even deadpan. "I have a supernatural ability to make things grow, only you weren't around to see it happen."

Instead of laughing, as any normal person might, Ally stared at him with an intensity that sent a frisson of worry through Morgan. How could Ally possibly know of his gift, or believe it if she'd heard the talk? Morgan wrapped the question of their powers' perceived impossibility around herself like a shield as she'd done throughout her life...but this time it had no soothing effect. She wanted to kick herself for encouraging Cade to use his gift where Ally could see the results.

Hobbling to the rickety gate, Ally entered the garden, where she proceeded to examine each plant in excruciating detail. "Impossible," she said, so quietly that Morgan couldn't tell if they'd been meant to overhear. Ally looked up, not at Cade, but at Morgan. "These are the same plants that were here this morning. This rosebush has identical scarring in the bark at its base. You can't possibly force growth that fast."

Unable to come up with a good response, Morgan looked at Cade, who cut in with, "She didn't do it, Ally."

"Well, *you've* been no help with answers, so I thought *she* might be," the redhead said. Morgan hid a smile, admiring the woman's pluck in spite of her own worry.

"I've given you all the information I can on Hope Creek and its growing conditions," he added.

"And none of it adds up!" Ally snapped. "I've got good soil and poor plants in some places, and average soil and—and—Jack's beanstalks in others!" She thrust a hand toward the bean plants at the garden's other end. When he didn't respond, she ran the hand through her hair, mussing it into an unruly russet cloud. "I'm out of ideas."

"Why don't you come riding in the mountains with Elsa and me this afternoon?" Morgan asked. "Maybe you could use the break. You've been working really hard."

From the corner of her eye, Morgan saw Cade staring at her with a what-are-you-going-to-tell-her look on his face.

"You know what? I'd like that. And I *could* use a break," Allyson answered, shooting a suspicious look at Kincade. She took Morgan's offered arm for support and they went out through the garden gate. As they left, Morgan shot an apologetic look back over her shoulder.

One thing was sure: in spite of all the puzzling and even frightening incidents that had happened to Allyson since coming to the ranch, she hadn't left yet. That meant either she was unusually driven in her quest to solve Hope Creek's problem, or a certain infuriating man had tweaked her interest enough to get her to stick around. Ally was more than a match for Cade's storm-cloud broodiness.

Morgan almost couldn't wait to see what happened next.

Chapter Thirteen

Ally clucked to her horse. The pretty palomino mare trotted faster up the mountain slope behind Morgan's Appaloosa and Elsa's borrowed quarter horse. A quick phone call to Brady Hart had secured Cade's family a few additional horses for operating the ranch until Smoky and Rumble Seat healed from their injuries. Allyson's own mount belonged to Brady's daughter, who was spending her summer abroad in England.

Ally sucked the crisp, fresh mountain air deep into her lungs. It revived her after her frustrating encounter with Kincade. Even the mystery of the fast-growing garden couldn't compare with the way his indifference had hurt.

After what they'd shared last night, part of her had expected—she didn't know what, but certainly not this coolness. He'd spoken as if they were mere acquaintances. Her pride prevented her from showing it, but that distant tone in his voice stung. It stood in sharp contrast with his husky words and steamy looks of last night. What had changed?

And what about those plants? She burned to know what was behind their rapid growth, and everyone's curious silence on the matter only drove her determination deeper. She *would* get to the bottom of this, whether they answered her questions outright or not.

Which was part of the reason she had agreed to this mountain ride. If Cade wouldn't talk to her, maybe his sisters would. At least, maybe Elsa. Morgan hadn't seemed any more willing to speak up than Kincade, though she'd been kinder about it.

Elsa swiveled in her saddle to look back at Ally. "Doing okay? How's your ankle?"

Ally tested the security of her foot in the stirrup. Snug enough, and riding was much easier than walking on it. "All right," she answered. "Where are we going?"

"To check on the cattle," said Elsa. She dropped back where the trail widened out and walked her horse alongside Ally's. "The pasture up here is still better than what we have down by the barns, so that's where we graze our herd."

Ally sat up straighter. Elsa had just handed her a perfect opening to broach the subject of the mystery plants. Coolly, she said, "I don't suppose you'd like to tell me what's going on around here, since nobody else will."

The sudden color in Elsa's cheeks made it clear that *something* was going on, all right, though the blonde woman didn't reply right away. She looked away, seeming to study the trail ahead, but Ally knew she was avoiding eye contact. "I don't think it's for me to say."

"It ought to be for *someone* to say, after the work I've done and the trouble we've had. I'm not getting very far with half the information. I'd like to have all the ammunition I can get to—" *To burn Julie's butt when she gets here.* "—to solve this," she finished. She smiled to take some of the harshness out of her words.

Elsa worried her lower lip in her teeth. She gave her horse an absent pat and then, with a wary glance at Morgan's back, the young woman leaned in her saddle until she and Ally were closer together. "Don't let Cade shut you out."

Ally blinked. Relationship advice?

Seeming to notice her confusion, Elsa added, "He thinks he doesn't need anyone. He does, but he doesn't want to admit it."

Just why did Elsa think Ally had come to Hope Creek? She thought for a moment, and then said delicately, "I don't think he hired me to date him."

"He needs you, Ally. And I'm not talking about dating. I mean, there's something about him—"

"Someone's been up here recently," Morgan said ahead of them.

Elsa and Ally looked up. Morgan had stopped her horse to stare at the trailside near a clump of bushes. Several of the branches had been broken.

"You mean besides Ethan?" Elsa called. "He has about as much grace as a heavyweight wrestler doing ballet."

"No—see the path they made?" Morgan pointed. "Come look."

Elsa spurred her horse forward and Ally followed. The women examined the haphazard trail broken through the undergrowth. "They went north," said Morgan. "A pretty straight track, as if they were making a short cut. Heading toward—"

"The cattle," Elsa said, alarm in her voice. She kicked the quarter horse's sides and the startled animal jumped forward into a canter down the trail. Morgan and Ally followed close behind.

Elsa and Morgan rode as fast as the trail allowed, no doubt worried for the fate of their livelihood. Ally, less familiar with the terrain, decided to slow her horse's gait to a trot. She trusted herself to find Cade's sisters along the clear path and by their animals' tracks in the dirt.

How had someone slipped onto the ranch yet again?

Cade and his brother and sisters couldn't monitor Hope Creek's every sprawling acre, she reminded herself. And in the mountains, who knew how many hiding places a person could use? Given the variety of game up here, someone could make themselves quite comfortable and avoid being seen or found for weeks.

Discomfited by the thought, she urged her horse on. She listened, but no sound of Cade's sisters reached her over the wind in the trees. The spicy pine-scented air and the *clop-clop* of her mare's hoofbeats filled her senses. The sheer *lack* of something suspicious worried her, but after several minutes she began to relax. Maybe Cade's sisters had found the trail of an animal.

And maybe pigs will dance in tutus. She nudged the mare into a faster trot.

About a half mile farther, the trail curved to the right and began to incline. Ally followed it. Her horse's hooves dug into the earth and the animal climbed obediently. By the time the trail leveled out, the mare panted with effort. Ally patted its neck and studied the ground.

Cade's sisters had come this way, all right. Fresh hoofprints, their toes pressed deep into the dirt, indicated the women were still riding fast. How much farther had they gone?

Clucking to her horse, Ally leaned forward in the saddle. The mare broke into a canter, and for a few moments Ally heard only the rhythmic hoofbeats.

A large, black shape loomed at the edges of her vision. Something enormous sprang out of the trees and onto the path ahead. The mare whinnied and jerked into a half-rear. Gasping, Ally pulled back on the reins. Her heartbeat pounded in her chest.

"What do you think you're doing?" demanded a familiar voice.

Cade.

Ally looked up. He sat astride a big paint horse, glaring at her. "You scared the life out of me!" she snapped.

He snatched the cheekstrap of the antsy mare's

bridle. The horse subsided at once. "Would have been a lot more scared if I had been our sneak attacker."

"I was following your sisters," she added. "It's not as if I'm up here waiting to be assaulted."

Without another word, he reined his horse around and started up the trail ahead of her.

Fuming, she followed. How dared he? First he'd given her the cold shoulder, and now he treated her like a child!

That's what you get for getting involved with a client, she scolded herself. *Did you expect him to treat you like a professional after that?* She shoved the nagging thoughts away at once. Something else was going on in that man's head, and she vowed to find out what.

****

Cade sensed Ally's affront as he rode up the trail ahead of her. He wanted to say something to smooth her ruffled feathers, but he kept his mouth shut. Better that she was angry with him than welcoming, because the way she smiled and kissed and touched him would lead to much more trouble down the road. A man trying to protect his family's abilities from discovery couldn't afford the luxury of an intimate relationship.

And right now, the danger to her was no better. Someone knew she was trying to fix Hope Creek's troubles, and that someone didn't want her to succeed. The faster she finished her business and got out of here, he told himself, the better.

He worried more than he'd let on about her safety. Up here in the mountains, far from any sort of help, she and his sisters could have been assaulted and he might not have known for hours.

He'd sulked and brooded and fumed while the women left on their ride up here. Finally he decided that no matter what his frustrations with Ally were, he'd rather keep her under his eagle eye than risk another incident that resulted in her injury. He almost welcomed a run-in with the bastard who had now attacked her twice. He'd even decided to do late-night inspections of the property in the hopes of catching the intruder returning to the ranch.

If he couldn't touch her, that son of a bitch sure wouldn't.

"Your sisters said they saw a trail through the woods," Ally said behind him.

He arched around in the saddle. "Why didn't you say that?"

"I was a little busy defending my decision to be up here."

"Too late now," he said. "I'm more worried about Morgan and Elsa."

"I'm not far behind them. Or I wasn't," she added.

A little farther on, they entered a clearing whose long grasses had been trampled flat. Most of the cows herded together at one end of the clearing, tails swishing, ears twitching, looking for all the world like they'd found paradise.

At the clearing's other edge, Elsa stood beside her horse. "We're all right, but some of the cows have gone missing," she said.

"Any sign of other people?" he called.

"Nothing that didn't get buried under hoofprints from the herd," said Elsa. She untied a rolled sleeping bag behind her horse's saddle, then began extracting items from her saddlebags. "I guess that's it, then. I'm camping up here for the night."

"No, you are not," he said as Morgan rode into the clearing. "I am staying here. You are staying down at the house where it's safe."

"I'm not a child anymore, Cade."

"And you're still safer at the house."

"What about you? You think you're going to be

safe from attack up here by yourself?"

Morgan rode closer. "Three cows, Kincade, and two calves. No sign of them, all the way up to Brady's property line."

"Diablo's going to have to wait," he said to Ally. When he saw the apprehension on her face, he bit back a stern order for her to join his sisters at the house. Guilt eroded his resolve. He couldn't keep dancing along this thin line with her. On one side lingered the scorching need to catch the threads of his gift and stitch them back together. On the other, a punishing self-recrimination for using a woman who deserved so much better.

Then he recalled the look in her eyes after the attack in the barn. The desperate fear when he'd snatched her from Rumble Seat's saddle as they fell.

The words came out before he realized he was speaking. "Ally, why don't you stay up here with me this afternoon?"

She gaped like a fish yanked out of its cozy pond.

So did Elsa, but with much more indignation. "Don't get all bent out of shape," he told her. "Ally has work to do up here—soil samples and surveys and whatnot—and I'm watching her. Leave your camp gear. We'll bring it back down."

"Come on, Elsa," said Morgan, reining her horse around and pointing him toward the trail home.

His youngest sister shot him a withering glare and dropped her gear. "Suit yourself." When she faced Ally, though, her expression changed, and a long look which Cade couldn't decipher passed between them. She vaulted into her saddle. "See you at the house."

His sisters cantered off. He watched until they disappeared into the trees. It occurred to him then that he'd be alone with Allyson for the entire afternoon and well into evening.

What a fool. How did he expect to keep his distance from her when he'd just signed his own permission slip to do otherwise?

You wanted to, taunted the devil on his shoulder. *You want this chance to get close to her again. That soft skin, that sinful strawberry scent that drives you mad—* He cut off the rest of the torturous thoughts before they forced him to forget his reasons to avoid her.

But his gaze wandered to her generous curves, to the burnished-red of the waning sunlight in her hair, to the pale skin of her slender arms as she lowered herself carefully from horseback to ground. She stood stork-legged, examining the soil with a studious eye. "Thanks."

"For what?"

"Giving me a chance to work."

He laughed. "What've you been doing since you got here? Sitting on your hands?"

"I just mean..." She sighed and slipped the reins over her horse's head, then tied them to a tree. "Once Julie gets here, I won't have much chance to...never mind."

"You're really worried about this lady, aren't you?" he asked. Watching her struggle to remove her horse's saddle, he walked forward and eased her aside to do it himself. "I trust your work, Ally. You should, too."

Bitterness filled her tone. "It's hard to trust your own data when it disagrees with itself at every turn. And it's hard to trust my own eyes. Sunflowers and gardens full of vegetation don't just spring into life in a matter of hours. How are they doing that? Who's playing the joke?"

"What does it matter how they did it? They did it," he said. "Your fertilizer—"

"No fertilizer on earth works that fast. I know it, and you know I know it." She bent and pulled a few vials, a pair of gloves, and a notebook from the horse's saddlebag.

He tried his best not to let his gaze rest on her perfect ass and failed miserably. Until he noticed the rigid line of her shoulders. "When you told Elsa to leave her camping gear," she asked, "did you mean for us to stay up here tonight?"

Her cautious, soft-spoken words shot straight to his groin. A shudder ran through him, and it was all he could do not to pull her up against his body. "I am," he said when he thought he could speak without letting the sudden, blinding need fill his voice.

She laid her equipment on a nearby boulder, then hobbled closer to him, so close he swore he felt the heat of her skin. In her eyes he saw not desire, but a level determination that set off sirens of warning in his head. "Then I am, too. I'm not playing anymore, Cade. I need to know what's going on around here."

"I didn't think you were playing before." He struggled to see past her curvaceous body, the flashing pulse at her throat, that damn strawberry smell. Couldn't she stop wearing the stuff? "Anyway," he forced out, "it's good you're staying up here where I can watch you. Too many people have been coming and going lately without my knowledge, and I don't need you to get hurt again."

She blew out an exasperated breath that fluttered a lock of flame-red hair into her eyes. "Thanks ever so much."

He wanted her bad enough already without that flush-cheeked, wayward-hair look. "Come on, Ally," he said, desperate for some distance. "Can't we just agree to finish this project without sniping at each other?" He grabbed his horse's reins and led him to the tree where her mare waited, the better to put some yardage between himself and the too-captivating redhead.

"I don't recall this being an argument," she said. "I have a job to do, and nothing's going to stand in my way of finishing it. Not burglars, not falls from horses...and sure as heck not you, Kincade Murphy."

The way she eyed him, pride and hurt and stubbornness all rolled into one magnetic package, Cade wanted to drop the pretense and tell her what he was. Or had been. Might still be. He cursed under his breath and shied away from the impulse. Family came first, he reminded himself. Their safety mattered more than his desires.

Even when those desires include a woman you can't stop needing? whispered his devil.

Oh, shut up, shut up, he pleaded with it, but he couldn't stop the steady flow of memories from his night with her. "Cattle," he spat, striding across the meadow to take a visual head count of the animals.

As he ticked off one broad, fuzzy nose after another, mounting dismay wrestled his stomach into knots. Morgan was right, damn it. Unless there was a huge pack of wolves up here that he didn't know about, he couldn't have lost five of his livestock in one fell swoop.

That, or his unknown visitor had taken to cattle thieving, too. Would the vulturing son of a bitch simply pick away at Cade's livelihood until only dry bones remained?

"Brady said he lost cows, too," Ally said behind him.

"When did you talk to Brady?"

"In town, at the café. After you...this morning," she said. She looked at him through her lashes. "I saw Maryanne, too."

"Bet that was a treat."

She seemed to want to say something further, though the line of her mouth went firm and thin as if she clamped her lips shut with an effort. At last, she turned away to her research equipment and began fussing with it.

He pivoted on his bootheel to scan the meadow, listening to the clink of glass and rustle of paper as they mingled with the whooshing mountain wind in the trees. Ally's voice reached his ears, too low for him to understand her words. "What did you say?"

He heard a click and she looked back over her shoulder. "Nothing. I was taking notes." She held a tiny voice recorder.

"You ought to sit down and rest that ankle," he said.

She lowered herself to a flattened boulder. "What are you going to do?"

"Take another circuit of the meadow, look for tracks Morgan and Elsa might have missed. I'll be within eyesight." Even as he spoke, he fought a piercing reluctance to move more than a few yards from her. He swept the clearing again, telling himself he was looking for the lost cows, not ensuring that the boulder on which she sat stood well into the open space of the field. He started to walk away, but with every step, the pull of her presence resisted it.

****

Ally turned to her notebook and began scribbling data onto a clean page. A half hour passed with no other sounds than those of the wind, birds, and shuffling cattle. A perfect, peaceful place to concentrate on all she needed to convey before Julie arrived.

Except that she'd only written half a page—and the rest of it, when she looked, was a series of doodles of a man on horseback. A man lounging in a chair beside a barn. A man with irresistibly-mussed hair. Embarrassed, and even more embarrassed that she *was* embarrassed, she flipped the page so fast it almost tore from its spiral binding. With a deep sigh she clicked her recorder on, then rattled off some environmental observations about the grazing area.

Good soil here. Better than the lower pastures, for certain. The grass had begun to get thready, but most was still long and green. Not as many flowers as she'd have liked this time of year, even in the places the cattle hadn't grazed. From time to time, her gaze strayed from the pages before her to the edges of the clearing.

When Kincade made it to the clearing's opposite border, a *boom* rocked the air. A mass of crows burst upward from several yards into the forest, protesting in loud, raucous voices. A few of the cows mooed and rolled their eyes. The whole gaggle of them bunched closer together.

Cade sprinted across the field as she jumped up from the rock. In seconds, he reached her side and thrust her between himself and the retreating flock of crows. "On your horse. Quick, quick!" He boosted her onto the mare's bare back and scrambled to untie the animal. The *boom* echoed again. Something screamed, eerie and shrill. The cattle bellowed and began shoving toward Ally's horse in one large, furry, reddish-brown surge.

Fear began to trickle under Ally's skin. "What is that?" she cried.

"A ready-made stampede," he said. He tried to reach his own horse, but two young cows barreled forward between him and his target. Ally heard a *whump.* Cade grunted and reeled back, almost falling.

With her breath stalled in her throat, she watched the scene. More cows rushed forward, following the first two. A huge spotted heifer smashed him in the shoulder. "Cade!"

He staggered and changed direction, launching himself at her horse. He leaped onto the animal's back behind her just as the bulk of the herd began to rush toward them, heading for the trail at the edge of the clearing. The earth trembled underneath them and the air rang with the herd's fearful mooing. Cade kicked the mare's sides and pointed her in the only direction left open—back toward the source of the noises.

A third *boom* tore the air, but this time it came from the direction the cows were running. Before Ally had time to process that, the confused herd turned and bolted again.

Straight toward them.

"Yah!" she shouted, jabbing her heels into the mare's sides. Pain flashed through her ankle. She ignored it.

The mare leaped forward and began running for a narrow gap between the trees. Behind them rolled the thundering of the herd's hoofbeats.

"We're not gonna make that," Cade called, pointing toward a fallen log wedged low in the space. "Ally, we're not gonna make it!"

"Hold on!" she yelled. She shouted to the mare again.

The palomino launched into the air just before the log. Cade swore and grabbed a fistful of the horse's mane. Ally felt the animal's hind hoof knock the log. The mare shuddered and landed heavily on the narrow track within the trees.

The ground shook as the herd of cows passed into the forest on both sides, avoiding the log and the deer track on which Ally and Cade had landed. The mare panted heavily and tossed her head.

"Get down," Ally said. "She may be hurt."

Cade did so and she followed. He checked the horse's legs and feet. "She's all right. Might have just clipped it with the edge of her hoof," Cade said. "No blood, no cuts. Doesn't look like any tender spots either. Brady's still going to skin me if he finds out what happened." He fell silent as the ruckus of the herd faded out.

"I'm more worried about the noises we heard," said Ally. She shrank closer to Kincade and peered into the trees. "And what was that scream?"

The warmth of his hand on her back soothed her rioting nerves. "My guess? Our intruder's back, and he's trying to kill us with an accidental trampling."

"It sounded like a mountain lion." Ally shivered, equal parts fear and the effect of Cade's touch.

"When you hear a real mountain lion, you'll know it. Come on." He helped her back onto the horse and climbed up behind her. Pressed close against her back, with his arms around her to handle the reins, he was a reassuring wall of safety.

Until she realized he had clucked the mare into motion along the deer track toward the first source of the noises. "Cade, I'm not so sure we should—"

He cut off her protest. "How many times is this guy going to waltz onto my property? Who's going to get hurt next, Ally? I'd rather it were him—and if I catch him, it will be."

She shivered at the barely-leashed anger in his voice and thanked her stars it wasn't directed at her. She knew without asking that Cade would defend his family and home until his dying breath. "What are you going to do if we find him?" she whispered.

"I'm going to get down and pound him flat. You're going to ride home as fast as this horse can carry you."

"Oh, no, I won't. What if there are more of them?"

"I'll deal with it." His hand came to rest over hers and he squeezed. "I don't doubt you'd take them all on single-handed, Ally, and I thank you for that. But you've already been hurt trying to save my home."

The gratitude and sincerity in his tone wrapped around her and soaked in. She opened her mouth to say something, but Cade clapped a hand over it and backed the horse into the brush.

Voices. Plural.

Terror poured through her. She huddled close against Cade's body. The thrill of his masculine warmth embracing her almost eclipsed her fear of the trespassers—but not quite.

She caught snatches of conversation. "It's in the clearing," said a man. "Watch your back, they're still up here somewhere." She couldn't identify the speaker, and by the silent scowl on Cade's face, he couldn't either.

Something rustled through the underbrush. Ally gripped the mare's reins in one white-knuckled fist, certain their unwanted guests could hear the fierce pounding of her heartbeat. The rustling neared their hiding place—*How flimsy it is, they could see us and the horse if they looked hard enough*—and she held her breath.

And then the sounds in the underbrush moved away.

She only dared to let out a breath after Cade turned the horse further into the woods along the deer track. "What would they want in the clearing?" she asked when she thought it safe to speak.

"The only *it* in the clearing is your stuff, unless they're hurting for a spare bedroll," Cade said. "Has someone other than you looked at that research? Did you already send it to the college?"

"Lots of it, yes. Julie's got it right now. I'm sure others have seen it. But Cade, as much as I don't like her, I can't see her sending people here to sabotage your ranch just to see me fail." That sort of thing was beyond even Julie...she thought.

Cade gave a murmur of agreement as he circled the mare toward the source of the booming noises they had heard. At last, they reached a wide trail and saw two sizable pits in the earth. The fringes of grass bordering them bore blackish scorch marks. "Quarter stick of dynamite, I'd say," he muttered.

"Let's go back," she whispered, half to herself. "I can't imagine what they would want with my notes. It's only soil tests and stuff."

He turned the horse around but pointed her along a more northerly route, circling the area. He scanned the ground for tracks. "Two people," he said, almost to himself. "On foot."

This far back into Cade's property? They had to have driven in on something that could handle the terrain. That, or they'd been up here a while. Ally pressed back against Cade's chest before she realized what she was doing.

"I'm not gonna let 'em hurt you again," he said. His arm curled around her for the briefest of squeezes and it sent another thrill through her. *Focus,* she scolded herself. *Intruders. With dynamite.* She sat up taller in the saddle, separating her body from his.

When they reached the clearing, his horse nickered to the mare. A few stray cows lingered at the edge of the clearing, but she heard some of them among the trees. And sure enough, her notebook and vials had disappeared.

Outrage filled her. "They can't stop me. They must know I'll only rewrite the notes. Half of it's already in Julie's hands."

Julie. Oh, merciful kittens. Even this little setback would look like a major catastrophe when Julie finished relaying it to Coonan. How could she excuse her missing notes with reports of invisible thieves?

"Well, that's it," Cade said, sliding down from the mare's back. "We're staying here tonight after all."

"We?" She'd thought he would send her packing back to the house since the very first explosion.

"Ethan's a good enough guard when he needs to be," he said, relieving her worries about his family, "but I'd rather you stay with me."

All other thoughts flew from her head. A shiver went through her, straight to her core. *He doesn't mean what you think. What you want him to mean. And you shouldn't want it either,* she told herself. *Especially not now.*

As he helped her down from the horse, he didn't meet her gaze, merely focused on the clearing as if looking for their unwanted guests. But his hands lingered on her waist, warm even through the fabric of her shirt, and she swore she felt him hesitate before he let go.

Chapter Fourteen

What the hell was he thinking? He ought to march her right back down to the house, where she'd have three pairs of eyes on her in case those creeping sons of bitches tried to attack her again. What made him think she'd be safer up here, at night, with miles of wild country around and no one but him to hear a cry for help?

He hadn't wanted Morgan or Elsa to stay up here, sure. And he knew he needed to. But if Allyson believed he only wanted her with him so he could protect her... Hell, he was fooling himself.

Even now, when she'd done no more than curl up in a patch of grass to stare at the emerging stars, he wanted to pull her against his body and kiss her breathless. The need to feel her cool skin against his left him almost lightheaded in its urgency. He opened his mouth to say her name and couldn't. Every time he formed the image of her in his head, it coupled with his own. In a bed. In a tiny room with pine-paneled walls and the faint, homey scents of horse and sawdust. And strawberries.

Her voice broke into his turbulent thoughts—quiet, but he caught the tension hovering in her question. "Do you think they'll come back tonight?"

"Not if they know what's good for them." He didn't add that he planned on staying awake all night, just to be sure.

That brought its own set of problems. She'd be lying right beside him, her body soft and yielding with slumber, and that glorious mane of flame-red hair spread out around her breath-stealing face.

It would be a long night.

A coyote yipped. Far off, another answered. With a smile, he noticed that she shifted just a bit closer. "They'll avoid us, don't worry. This clearing's full of the scent of human."

"Do you get wolves up here?" she asked.

"Occasionally. They'll leave us alone, too."

Crickets began their nightly song. "A regular wildlife preserve, isn't it?" she asked.

"Yep. Part of the reason I don't want to let this place go." He kept his voice even, though anguish strained to fill his words.

"I'm so sorry about my research getting stolen, Cade. I swear it won't set me back."

"I know." The anguish did come now, and he waited until it passed to speak again. "You've got to be tired. Get some rest. We'll track the rest of the cows in the morning, and then head down for breakfast."

She was silent for a few moments. Finally he heard her shuffling a few feet away. "Cade, what do you have in your saddlebags?"

The question caught him off guard. "A couple pairs of gloves, some fence repair tools. A few sandwich bags of washers and bolts. Why?"

"May I have the bags?"

"Sure," he said, curious now. What on earth could she need with sandwich bags? But he got to his feet and went to his horse's saddle, where he extracted them and dumped the hardware back into the saddlebags. He brought the fistful of bags to her, five or six of them.

Grinning, she turned them inside out. "It's not perfect procedure, but under the circumstances, I'll take what I can get. Let's see those thieving sneaks stop me." She scooped up a handful of soil using the bag as a scoop, then turned the bag right side out again and zipped the closure shut. "Who needs vials?"

Warm admiration filled him. His Ally wasn't one for cringing from a challenge.

His?

Oh, Cade, he heard Morgan say in his head, almost as if his sister were there to shake her head in disapproval.

He reeled away from Ally on the pretense of checking her horse again. The mare showed no signs of injury from her wild gallop and jump to safety. A good horse. Brady must be proud to own such an animal. Cade rubbed her twitching velvet nose and she butted her head against his chest.

His own mount grazed in the meadow. He stalked through the grass to the gelding's side and rubbed its forehead. "Everything's easy for you, isn't it, Dancer?" he murmured. "You've seen and done it all." The gelding whiskered over Cade's fingers, snuffling for treats. Finding none, he returned to grazing.

"He's beautiful," came Ally's voice.

Cade turned to find her hobbling toward them. She laid a hand on the gelding's side, tracing the light-and-dark pattern of his coloring. "I've never seen such a pretty horse, except for Diablo."

"Diablo's a mean-tempered old coot," Cade said, more out of habit than with any feeling. Truly, the stallion seemed fine during Ally's forced-proximity experiment. Maybe she'd missed her calling as a horse trainer.

For a few moments, he listened to the sounds of the night animals and insects, hardly noticing the time as it passed. Awareness of the woman beside him filled his senses until he longed to touch her. Watching her stroke the gelding's hide, he made out the shadowy curves of her cheek and nose. Pale skin glowing in the starlight, she seemed as ephemeral and otherworldly as a goddess of the forest.

Maybe her calling was simply to bewitch him. In her short time at Hope Creek, she'd worked under his skin until he thought of little else. Even his brother and sisters seemed to welcome her with open arms, in spite of the secret they worked so hard to keep.

Cade left her side long enough to make a few circuits of the clearing, never leaving eye contact with her. Nothing disturbed the peace, but it gave him something to do. Something to distract him from the way he needed to be close to her. When he returned, Ally was scratching the gelding's neck and murmuring in a low, musical tone that skipped over Cade's skin and left a sizzling trail.

"I think," she said at last, "that tomorrow I'm going to finish my official report to the college."

Disappointment rattled him. Did that mean she planned to end her assignment even earlier? His devil howled at the very idea...but he had no right to keep her here. He tried for a casual voice. "What's your final assessment then, Miss Hamilton?"

"I don't think I'm going to find anything wrong with the property, Cade. And I think you know that, too." She didn't sound angry...just resigned. Somehow that bothered him. He didn't want her to give up. Part of him, a small but nagging part, wanted her to keep trying until she discovered the unlikely truth.

Unable to stop himself, he touched a lock of her hair, letting it slip through his fingers until it fell back into place. "You aren't quitting because of Julie, are you?"

Her eyes met his with no trace of suspicion or calculation. "No. You've got something going on here that I...I can't know about. I see it in your face."

How could she see that? His need for her eclipsed every other thought in his head when he looked at her. "Ally," he began, without knowing what else to say. Even in the darkness he saw sadness in her eyes. Wanting to erase it, he stepped forward and kissed her.

She made a soft noise and leaned into him, her body feather-light against his own. She pressed still closer. He winced, tried to jerk back, to get control of himself...but it was too late. He gave himself up for lost and his internal devil snarled with glee.

She wound her fingers through his hair, pulling him toward her for another kiss that he had no prayer of resisting.

He lifted the hem of her shirt to stroke the silk-soft skin underneath. She sighed and raised her chin, allowing his kisses to wander to her throat where he inhaled her addicting strawberry scent.

He towed her toward the bedroll and she made no protest. They made love with slow tenderness, as if each of them somehow knew they'd never get another chance at this. He traced each curve of her body, committing them to memory. And when they peaked together and his lost power surged through his body, he let it go to focus instead on the ecstasy in her eyes.

Afterward, he let her have the sleeping bag for the rest of the night, with the excuse that he'd be up often to check on the herd and didn't want to disturb her. But when she closed her eyes and her breathing evened out into slumber, he just watched her. Only when the birds began to sing and the sky picked up the first pale threads of pink and yellow, did he notice that he hadn't thought of his power once all night.

When she woke, he was already busy tacking up the horses. He managed a smile. "Ready to herd some cattle? We've got a lot to do today, so we'd better get an early start."

"You didn't sleep at all, did you?"

He examined the cinch of his horse's saddle.

"That sleeping bag wasn't going to hold both of us anyway."

She didn't answer, and he avoided looking back to gauge her expression. Dangerous waters there.

The grass-muffled sound of her footsteps came to a stop behind him. "Julie will be here today," she said. He heard the uneasiness under the forced-calm tone.

"Yep," he answered. Still avoiding eye contact, he cupped his hands to help her into her saddle.

She laid a hand on his shoulder and paused. He sensed the struggle within her through that small point of contact, but she vaulted into the saddle without speaking.

As soon as she was settled on her horse, he packed up the few things they'd spread out for the night, then went to his own mount.

Herding the cattle took his mind off anything else, and he found himself grateful. Their search brought them deeper into the forest, though he made sure Ally was never farther from him than shouting distance. He'd take no chances with her safety anymore. They found the last few stragglers in another tiny clearing about half a mile away and herded the lot back toward the clearing where they'd slept.

Ally gasped. He looked up with alarm, expecting to be confronted by their trespassers, but found a sweep of color. The cattle waded through a sea of wildflowers that hadn't been there two hours before.

"I don't believe it," she whispered. She stayed silent after that. She didn't even look at him.

With a huge effort, he kept working, pressing the cattle onward through the clearing. Ally seemed to come back to herself and helped round up the stragglers, though she still avoided his gaze. Even when the tallest of the flower stalks brushed her legs she said nothing, riding ahead without so much as a nod toward him.

He struggled to find something to say, but talk seemed to require acknowledgement of the obvious and undeniable evidence of something fishy going on at Hope Creek. How the hell had he thought he could get her help restoring his gift and then deny the results if—*when*—they appeared?

When he passed a tree or shrub growing tall enough to reach from horseback, he let his fingers trail over it as casually as possible. His power fizzed, sputtered, died, and sputtered again. Every few tries, the plant flushed just a little greener. Surprise warred with disappointment and—in varying measures, but growing stronger every second—regret.

They went on, herding the cows along the path to the lower lands nearer the house. Each minute that passed brought him closer to an admission he didn't want to make: he needed to tell her to go. Without letting her finish her assignment. Without getting his power back. Without ever touching her again. He couldn't risk exposure of his family's powers. The whole thing had been folly.

And still he wanted to open his mouth and confess everything, just to hear her speak to him— even in anger. Her silence tortured him. He would have given anything, traded anything, to know what was going through her head right now.

When they reached the low pastures, Ethan met them at the gate and helped usher the cattle inside. He must have seen the gloom on Cade's face, because his own expression darkened. "What now?"

"We didn't find anyone up there, although we did run across some of their calling cards. We're still missing a few cows."

"This is outright theft, Cade. Shouldn't we get the sheriff involved?"

Cade considered that. An oddly thoughtful

statement, for Ethan. Maybe his younger brother was starting to think of people other than himself. Or he thought they weren't getting anywhere with Ally's help, and the ranch would be sold off by next week.

Except they were getting somewhere.

He scanned the pasture for Ally. She had ridden along the fence toward the opposite gate, seeming content to walk her horse back to the barn without him. Cade lowered his voice. "I'm going to tell her to leave."

"You can't be serious." Ethan pushed the brim of his hat back and crossed his arms on the fence's top rail. "What the hell was all that work and bitching for if you're just going to give up?"

"It's back, Ethan." Cade prepared himself for a round of torment. Ethan would know exactly why Cade thought his power had returned.

The harping didn't come. His brother's cat-gold eyes remained sharp and scrutinous, but somehow unreadable. "Permanently?"

"I don't know. Maybe not. There're flowers up there that weren't, yesterday. The feeling comes and goes."

"What're you gonna do if it disappears again? Just call her back like a yo-yo?"

"I don't know," Cade snapped. "I'm not asking her back. If it goes again, it stays gone."

Ethan muttered something Cade didn't hear, and he couldn't decipher it by his brother's expression because Ethan had looked away. When he returned his gaze to Cade's, any hint of what bothered him had vanished. "She's gonna be hurt."

"Since when do you care about women's feelings?"

"We have two sisters." The pissant gleam came back into his brother's eyes. "If I don't look like I care, I don't hear the end of it."

189

"Don't say anything to Morgan or Elsa. They won't understand."

"I don't either," Ethan pointed out. "You were so damn insistent on getting your power back, and now you're junking the idea of keeping it."

"Quit worrying. I'll find another way to save the ranch."

"I don't give a damn about Hope Creek," Ethan snarled.

Outrage and stung pride blasted through Cade's body. If he hadn't been astride the horse, he would have punched his brother then and there. It took all his resolve to keep his feet in the stirrups. He didn't even trust himself to speak.

Sighing, Ethan tugged his hat down lower. "I do care, Cade, but not like you. We all know you'd die for this place."

The snarling anger mellowed a little. Cade thought about how hard he'd held on to this patch of land, how much it meant to him. But instead of picturing the rolling green hills and fields of his home, he saw a pair of gray eyes framed by a beautiful, pale face and long, fiery-red hair. Then he saw that face filled with hurt when he ordered her to leave. "Where are you going with this, Ethan?" he growled.

"Nowhere. Apparently." His brother jerked his shoulders and stalked away toward the horse barn.

****

When Ally entered the house, the smell of Italian food greeted her and her mouth watered. She'd spent a summer internship in New York City, where the Italian fare was second only to that found in the mother country. The luscious scent wafting toward her smelled like the genuine article.

Morgan sure knew how to cook. Why was she wasting her talents here in Montana, miles from anywhere? Any five-star restaurant would commit homicide to get their hands on her culinary skills.

Ally hobbled into the kitchen, where she found Morgan setting a pan of bubbling lasagna on the stove. Beside it rested a dish that looked like dessert—something crumbly and golden-brown that smelled so good she wanted to start with that first.

Elsa stood at the sink surveying the pan of lasagna and the dessert beside it. "Is this going to be enough, Morgan?"

"That's plenty. I'm not going to truck it all back if it's not eaten."

"Nobody's going to leave a single crumb," Elsa assured her.

"We'll see about that," said Morgan, but Ally spied a smile on the woman's lips. She pulled a covered plate from the microwave. "Glad you're back safe. We made omelets. I didn't even have to reheat it."

Ally thanked her and dug in, realizing only now how hungry she'd been. Herding was hard work. Her respect for Cade and his family rose several degrees.

Elsa handed her sister a box of plastic wrap to cover the still-tempting dessert on the stove. "Ready to brave the church potluck, Ally?"

Dismayed, she sat at the table. "That's today?"

The young woman's expression clouded over. "I suppose you could stay here if you want..."

"No, no. That's not what I meant. I meant..." What *did* she mean? Her time at Hope Creek was slipping away, and Julie would be here soon. Today, in fact. How would it look if she found Ally spending hours at social events instead of working? What would she report to Coonan?

"There'll be dancing," Elsa said. Then her gaze shifted to Ally's cane, leaning against the table. "Oh. But you won't want to, will you?"

A sudden vision swamped Ally of dancing in Kincade's strong arms. The smile on his face. The steamy look in his eyes. The way everything else blurred out when he was near.

In a rush, she longed to be free of the cane. To have an excuse to be seen in his arms instead of stealing moments away from observers. Could it be so terrible if they were together?

What about after she finished her assignment?

A new resolve fired her blood. She'd finish it, all right. She'd find a way around all the conflicting data and give the department the best report in history. She'd—

"Ally?"

Cade's voice. He was coming down the hall into the kitchen, almost like a sign. It was so simple. She almost laughed. What had she been worried about?

He stalked into the living room, but didn't continue to the kitchen. "I need to talk to you." He angled his head toward his bedroom.

She rose from her breakfast and followed him, trying and failing to look casual. She knew she lacked the ability to hide strong emotions behind an impassable mask. It didn't matter anymore. Soon she'd have no reason to hide the way she felt about him.

He pushed open his door. She had time only for a quick impression of rugged cedar-log furniture and denim blue before he turned on her with a grim expression. "I'm asking you to go home, Ally."

Her mouth fell open, but she couldn't seem to make it form words. Her skin flushed cold, then hot, then cold again. She leaned on her cane until the heel of her hand hurt—but nothing felt worse than the hole opening in her chest. As if everything good in her life had been sucked out of that once-warm, sunny spot and left an aching vacuum.

Insult filled the hole first. "How can you call this off right when you know Julie's about to come and look over my shoulder? I've already done all this work!"

He rubbed a hand through his already-wild hair. "It's not about you," he said. "Ally, I just don't think this is going to fix my problem." He met her gaze for the briefest of seconds, and torture flashed in his eyes before he looked away.

"Cade. What is it?" She dared a touch on his arm and found it hard as granite.

"You can't help me, Ally." His tone said *I won't let you help me.*

Staring him down, forcing him to make eye contact, she said, "The sunflowers. The garden. The wildflowers this morning. I'm not stupid—"

"I never—*never*—even implied that," he said, so forcefully that she took a step back. His eyes blazed with a glimpse of the passion and conviction she'd felt in him last night. Her body burned in response, even through her frustration.

She shook off the reaction and tried to focus. "Tell me what's going on. I deserve it. You know I do."

"You deserve a damn sight more than that, but it doesn't change my decision." He sighed and turned away to his dresser. "When Julie comes, I'm telling her we've finished everything that can be done here at the ranch. I'll write you whatever letters you need."

He might as well have slapped her across the face and pushed her out the door. Shaking with hurt and anger, she hobbled out of the room.

Elsa met her in the kitchen, frowning over Ally's shoulder. "He's such an idiot."

Surprise swept in underneath her raw feelings. It was probably the least charitable thing she'd ever heard Elsa say, but she couldn't bring herself to disagree.

"I'm sorry I listened," Elsa said. She took Ally's free hand, and her voice lowered so that Ally had to lean forward to hear. "He has no idea how much he needs you. In more ways than he thinks. You're good for him. Don't think you're not."

"How about whether or not *he's* good for *me*?" She pulled her hand from Elsa's. "It doesn't matter. I'm done here."

"At least come eat something at the picnic. All that food, you must be hungry—"

"No, thank you. I think I'll stay to pack my things and get ready to leave when Julie arrives. She's probably already on her way." *How could he? How* could *he?* she cried silently. Had this been nothing more than a fling for him? A little fun with the hired help? She struggled to reconcile this callous man with the one who had scolded her about not believing in herself.

She heard the door swing open behind her and forced away the tears wanting to spill over. She raised her head and thumped down the hall, stiff-backed and silent. No way would she let him see her crying.

She'd wait until he left.

Chapter Fifteen

There were exactly fifty-three ways to call yourself an idiot. Cade used every single one while the residents of Sagerton oohed and aahed over Morgan's dishes at the potluck supper.

Asking Ally to leave had pained him, taken more resolve than he thought he had—but it didn't wrench in his belly half as much as doing so without letting her finish her assignment. He believed in her. She was smart. Determined. She might even have saved his ranch her own way, if they'd only had time to find out.

The hurt in her eyes— Hell, he may as well have kicked a kitten. What a jerk. Couldn't have a single good thing without screwing it all up.

He wished he hadn't said anything at all.

After a few minutes of pushing scalloped potatoes around his plate, he gave up and turned to his coffee.

From his seat at a picnic table, he watched the people on the dance floor under the gazebo, their faces shining under the strings of lights lining the eaves. High school kids staring at each other with stars in their eyes. Older couples he'd known all his life. Even Maryanne seemed to glow as her boyfriend raised her hands to his lips and kissed them. She beamed and waved as he slipped away and went somewhere.

Everybody was so damned happy, he felt worse.

He had to admit several of the residents seemed pleased—or at least unsurprised—to see them in town. Even Bea and Viola couldn't find anything frosty to say. They were too busy doling out cups of lemonade and punch. Many of the people asked after Ally, and Cade couldn't bring himself to do more than mutter that she hadn't felt well enough to come.

No one hesitated to absorb Cade and his family back into their social doings. Morgan's food almost hadn't hit the table before people began digging in. Ethan tossed horseshoes with some of the younger guys. Elsa danced with a couple of the men who'd been watching her since their arrival. His little sister drew a lot more stares than when she was in pigtails. When had she grown up and gotten so...noticeable?

"Evenin', Cade." Jim Sagerton tipped his hat and sat down.

"Hi, Jim. Feeling better?" With an inward groan, Cade remembered his talk with Maryanne. He hated being a busybody. Sagerton had enough of those already. But a promise was a promise. "Listen, your daughter's been worried about your health ever since your hospitalization."

"Aw, I know all that, Cade. 'Take your medicine. Eat better. You gotta start exercisin'.' Almost like having my wife back." Jim stopped talking then, and for an instant Cade saw how much he missed the woman he'd always bellowed about while she was alive.

"Well, she asked me to talk to you," added Cade, "and it wouldn't be Maryanne if she wasn't interfering with something."

"She can't help it. It's her mama's genes." Jim adjusted the fit of his broad-brimmed hat. "Been meanin' to talk to you private, son. I know you been strugglin' with that ranch a while."

"Jim—"

"Don't get all uppity about your pride. Listen to what I got to say." The mayor propped his elbows on the table. "I've got some money put by that I've been savin' for investments. And I want to invest it in Hope Creek's livestock."

Confusion. Suspicion. Surprise. More confusion. "Why would you do a thing like that now?"

"Because my damnfool daughter begged me not to have that stallion put down. I didn't realize how bad off you were gettin' until I visited the other day." He waved to hand to stall Cade's protests. "I know all about you think you don't need anybody, but truth is, this town needs you. We need honest people running honest businesses, and I'm not gonna let yours sink. You raise good cattle and great horses. I mean to make sure you keep doing it. It ain't a handout. It's an investment."

Cade's pride warred with unexpected warmth. He and the mayor had always gotten along well, but he'd never have anticipated this. For one wonderful minute, he let himself hope.

But even truckloads of money wouldn't solve the bigger problem. His crops were still dying. His livelihood would still fail under the weight of his broken power.

He was killing his own land by being there.

He flexed his hands under the table. If only he knew what had caused the reversal of his power, he could fix it. Trying to hide his grief, he said, "Thanks, Jim. I'll think about it."

"You do that, son. Say hello to that pretty lady you got workin' for you when you get home." Jim stood up, shook Cade's hand, then ambled away.

Alone, Cade studied his palms. How did a man fix something broken when he couldn't see the break? The only times his power surfaced had been those moments with Ally. He couldn't use her like that. She'd been so determined, so willing to help him. Even when she said nothing, he felt her buoyant presence. And she never let him get into a funk about his plight when she was around. She'd been a better friend to him in this past week than most people were in a lifetime.

"Cade Murphy, you haven't touched a bite of my rhubarb pie." Rose Conklin appeared on the other side of the table, grinning down at him. He dug for an answering smile, but it didn't sit well on his face.

The older woman lowered herself to the weathered bench with a soft grunt. "You got a case of redhead, boy, and you ain't gonna get rid of it."

"What makes you so sure my problem is Ally?" He busied himself tossing back the rest of his now-cold coffee.

"She's not here, is she? And don't give me that malarkey about her bein' sick. You don't fool me worth a damn, and you never did." She curled a hand behind his neck and tugged him closer. The touch startled him, but he didn't resist it. She swatted his cheek. "I never cared what you were, and she doesn't either. You mind that."

Alarm bells clanged along his nerves. "What am I, then?" he asked in his most casual tone.

She laughed. "A damn good farmer."

Her answer startled a chuckle out of him. He rubbed his thumb over the lip of the coffee cup. "Wish I could believe you, Rose."

"Elsa told me what you're like around that young woman—"

"Elsa should mind her own business."

"—and I've seen her for myself. You're smitten, the both of you."

"Is that so?"

"Why else would you be hangin' a puss at this table with an old crank like me, 'stead of dancing or eating or throwin' shoes? You're sick in love with her."

He gave a quiet, self-mocking laugh and examined the torn edge of his paper plate. Rose saw too much for her own good. Or *his* own, anyway.

"She's gonna go back to Bozeman tomorrow and finish her report on your place, and you're never gonna hear from her again," Rose added. "What're you gonna do when she meets a man who wants her the way you do? Grab her while you can, boy. She may not be there when you look again."

The thought of her with another man harpooned him in the belly. Until now, he'd consciously avoided such an image. He squeezed the coffee cup until his knuckles went white. His devil gave a territorial snarl and began stabbing him with a pointy little mental finger.

God knew it would happen. She had brains. She had compassion. She had guts. She was more than any power he possessed. And damn if he could stomach letting any other man wake up next to her beautiful face for the rest of his life.

Cade shot to his feet. "Gotta go, Rose."

She chuckled. "Damn right, you do. Get outta here. I'll send a pie home with your family."

He jogged to his battered truck and opened the door with a rusty screech, then slid into the cab and keyed the engine.

Thirty miles to home. His old truck wouldn't make it there in less than forty-five minutes even if he pushed it. What if Julie arrived and they left before he got there? Would Ally hate him forever for pushing her away? How stupid he'd been.

As soon as he hit the highway, Cade slammed on the accelerator.

****

Fighting tears, Ally laid her suitcase in the trunk of her sedan. It hardly seemed like she'd spent almost a week here.

"Do you have anything else?" Julie asked from the horse barn doorway. She stood with crossed arms and a frown of impatience. She seemed to want

199

to leave Hope Creek as fast as possible, unlike Ally, who kept finding excuses to linger. She'd forgotten this chart or that book, a sock, a hairbrush. A granola bar she stuffed in her shirt pocket.

"That's everything," she admitted. "I've given you all my research, and you saw the results we've gotten on my testing. All that's left is getting Bailey."

Julie spared the sunset-washed garden an indifferent glance before disappearing back into the barn. She had taken few notes on her arrival. Ally supposed it didn't matter. Julie would give the department her own opinion, regardless of visual proof. Ally wanted to be glad Cade wasn't here, that Julie couldn't see them together and guess at their relationship...but she felt only crushing pain where her heart used to be.

He didn't want her. He thought she'd failed him. Her work didn't matter, and she didn't either.

She closed her trunk, then heard the rumble of a sliding stall door followed by gleeful yapping. "Get back here!" came Julie's shout.

A cold chill fluttered down Ally's back. "Oh, no," she breathed.

A split second later, Bailey raced out the open loading door into the main paddock. Julie scrambled along behind in her miniskirt and heels. "Ooh, you little—"

Diablo saw them from his corner of the pasture and rounded on them, galloping fast. Stumbling, trying to ignore the pain in her ankle, Ally hurried toward the fence and clambered over it. "Get back!" she yelled to Julie.

The woman shrieked at sight of the stallion racing toward them and cowered behind Ally. Bailey barked and kept running right for the horse, too far away for Ally to catch him. Stricken, she raised her hands. "No! Bailey! Bailey!" The ground shook as the stallion thundered nearer. She wanted to close her eyes, couldn't bear to watch her dog be killed.

But Diablo stopped.

He skidded to a halt in the long, weedy grass right before Bailey, who leaped in circles like a mad dervish. The stallion snorted and his ears came forward.

And the two animals touched noses.

Bailey yipped again and circled round and round the stallion's feet. Diablo shook his mane and went back to grazing.

Ally covered her mouth with both hands. Tears burned in her eyes.

"What now?" Julie whispered behind her.

"Shh-h-h-h," Ally warned. "Get back into the barn."

"I'll do better than that. I'm starting back to Bozeman. I've seen enough here." Distaste dripped from every syllable.

Ally heard rustling in the grass, growing fainter, and then nothing until a car door slammed and the vehicle zoomed off down the driveway. Julie had been at the ranch a mere two hours.

Ally realized then how different they were. Julie would never love fieldwork. And Ally lived for it. She no longer cared what job the department gave her, as long as she could breathe mountain air and hear the wind in the grass. See everyday magic in nature's beauty. In the sight of a horse in its pasture, making friends.

She backed toward the barn doorway. She'd left her cane in the bunkroom, and she stumbled through the grass. "Bailey," she called when she reached the pavement of the breezeway just inside the arch. "Come."

Diablo raised his head and watched her. The puppy gamboled around his feet. She held her breath, fearing for Bailey, praying he'd decide to come to her.

But he didn't. Diablo did.

The stallion swished his tail once and walked toward her. She froze as Bailey darted after the horse, worried she'd been wrong about her dog's safety—but Diablo came to a stop in front of her, half inside the barn.

When Ally reached out to the stallion, her hand trembled. The stallion gave a soft sigh through his nostrils, and then her fingers brushed his velvet muzzle. "H-Hi, big boy," she whispered.

He lowered his head, leaning into her as she scratched between his ears. Trusting her.

Awash in wonder, she pulled the granola bar from her pocket and offered it to the stallion on her palm. Diablo's lips swept across her skin and the treat disappeared. He crunched a few times and nosed her shirt for more.

This time she let the tears come, and she laughed through them until she cried again. If only Cade were here to see this.

"Hello, Miss Hamilton," came a voice.

She wiped her tears and arched around. Paul Riegel leaned against a stall door in the breezeway. "Hello," she answered. "Are you looking for Kincade? Everyone's at the picnic."

"Yes, I know that," he said in a strange, detached tone.

The first pulse of apprehension shot through Ally's nerve endings. "What can I do for you?" Dimly she heard Bailey trot into the barn. The dog snuffled around her feet, then went to Paul and did the same.

Paul's gaze shifted to the bunkroom. "The place looks cleaned out. Are you leaving without saying goodbye?"

The word almost brought her to tears again, echoing through the painful hollow in her chest. "I've already said it," she responded, trying to drain her voice of any inflection. Her emotions were too raw, too personal, too close to the surface. She felt like tissue paper. Any more words might tear her in two, but they refused to be stopped. "We were so close," she whispered.

"Close to what?"

"To fixing the problem. The garden is blooming. There are whole fields with flowers up in the mountains. Whatever we did, it's working. And he doesn't want me to finish. I don't understand."

Paul stared out the breezeway door and across the driveway toward the garden. He came away from the stall door and stood square on his feet. The motion brought him closer. "I don't either," he murmured. "Can he be healing?"

"Excuse me?"

He seemed to have forgotten her. "Maybe Maryanne was wrong."

"I'm sorry, I don't know what you mean," she said.

He turned back to her. "You *are* leaving." It wasn't a question.

"Yes. And it's all so stupid." The words tumbled out of her. "We were just starting to improve the place. I don't know what it was, but every time we worked together, things just...got better. Something was going right."

"It's you," Paul said, and his eyes had gone cold and wild. He stomped forward and seized her by the shoulders.

"What are you— Let go!" she demanded, wrestling against his grip and failing. Behind her, Diablo nickered and stamped a hoof.

"You!" he snarled, shaking her. "I've worked too damn hard setting this up, getting the bank to close them down—"

"You *what*?" Outrage flooded her, lending her the strength to throw his arms off. "How could you?

How dare you!"

"Several million dollars makes a man dare quite a lot," he said through his teeth. "This land is worth more than anything he and his stupid neighbor can put on it. Prime property for a planned housing development. Murphy's not going to pull a miracle cure at the last minute. And you're sure as hell not going to help him."

Her cheek throbbed with a remembered slap. Paul had attacked her that first night. Paul and his hired thugs had been sneaking onto the property, stealing cows and trying to destroy Cade's livelihood. "You—you— Get off this ranch!" she shouted, boiling with fury.

"You first." Paul's hands went for her throat.

A squeal of wrath burst into the air. A huge black shape loomed at her side, lunging for him. Diablo, teeth bared, ears flat. He half-reared and struck out with his forehoofs, forcing Paul back against the opposite stall door. Bailey started barking fit to alarm the next county.

Ally twisted, stifling a moan at the pain in her ankle. Using a pipe on the wall for leverage, she scrambled onto the stallion's back. She didn't care that he was unridable. She'd take her chances.

The horse didn't even seem to notice. His hoofs struck again, hitting the stall door just as Paul dodged out of the way. The man rushed for the open loading door at the far end, and Ally saw an unfamiliar all-terrain vehicle silhouetted in the fading light.

Paul ran for it. Diablo gave chase with a shriek of equine rage. Ally pulled on the stallion's mane, trying to turn him around and get to the bunkroom phone, but she may as well have been a fly on his back. As he gained speed, she gave up trying to stop him and flung her arms around his neck.

Paul leaped onto the four-wheeler and punched

the engine. The vehicle revved and skidded away toward the pasture, heading for a gate that stood open.

Then she saw the gun.

She screamed and tried again to get Diablo to stop, but he plunged ahead like a locomotive. His muscles bunched, released, bunched again. His strides devoured the ground, bringing them closer to Paul with each step. With a whimper of terror, Ally shrank against the stallion's neck.

The gunshot crashed through her ears and echoed off the mountainsides. She heard the crack of splintering wood behind her. Bailey's howls faded as they chased Paul through the gate into the foothills.

The four-wheeler veered right and Paul took aim again. Tears burned down Ally's cheeks. She clung to Diablo in desperation. "Go, go, please go!" she sobbed.

Diablo's stride lengthened even further as pelted up the mountain slope. They flashed past Paul as another gunshot tore the air apart. She didn't dare look back. Diablo's breath churned like a bellows.

A third gunshot zinged past them, smacking a tree that showered needles onto them. Fear slammed her heart against her ribcage with jackhammer speed. *Runrunrunrunrun,* it pounded out. Stars splashed before her vision. She hugged the horse's sweaty neck, begging the fates not to let her fall off. Each stride jostled her precarious hold. Even when the four-wheeler's motor revved behind them, she couldn't look.

Tree branches whipped against her. She squeezed closer to the stallion's neck. How far to Brady's land? Would anyone be there to help her? Would she even reach it if she kept going in this direction? Oh, God, she could be killed and no one would find her up here.

She'd never see Cade again.

Choking with grief, she tried to see where the stallion was taking them, but inky darkness had spread over the mountain forest and engulfed any recognizable shapes. The sound of the four-wheeler dimmed, muffled in the dense trees. She could no longer judge its direction. Was it closer? Farther away?

On and on the stallion ran, a wild hurtle through shapeless shadows and grasping branches that tore at her shirtsleeves. Her arms shook. Her fingers slipped on his sweaty hide. She listened for the revving motor until her head ached, but the forest had swallowed it, too.

Diablo's hindquarters bunched. She had time for one bitten-off gasp before he launched himself into starlight.

The stallion soared into the air over a yawning gully. Ally's stomach plunged and her hands came loose. For a moment, she went weightless and breathless.

Diablo landed. Pain smashed through her body. She swooped forward over his neck and slammed into something hard. Darkness crashed down around her.

Chapter Sixteen

Cade jerked the gearshift into park and sprang out of the truck, leaving it running in his haste. Ally's car was still in the driveway. She hadn't left. She hadn't left. She hadn't left.

He jogged into the barn. "Ally!"

The moment he entered the breezeway, a blazing sense of *wrong* washed over him. Bailey cowered near the bunkroom door, shaking and whimpering with his tail tucked between his legs.

Cade rushed toward the bunkroom door and shoved it open. Nothing was disturbed. He searched inside, but found no trace of her. "Ally?" he yelled, alarmed now.

No answer.

Racing out of the bunkroom, he searched the barn, calling her. Christ, why had he left her here alone? Had those men come back in his absence to attack her again? Cade choked back an agonized snarl. *God, anything but her. Take the damn ranch.*

He left the bunkroom and scooped Bailey up. The pup huddled in his arms and he scratched its ears in a distracted effort to comfort it. "Allyson!" Cade shouted. The breezeway resounded with a forlorn echo. He rushed outside.

In the barn's floodlight, he saw two parallel tracks of torn earth streaking away toward the open pasture gate. Between them, crossing over them, was a set of hoofprints. Then he realized that, before they'd left for the picnic, he'd released Diablo into the pasture. *What the hell?*

With no time for questions, he rounded back to

Dancer's stall. He lowered Bailey to the floor and snatched the horse's tack. "I need you, boy," he said to the horse. The gelding lowered his head to accept the bridle. True to his name, the old paint shifted on his toes, impatient to be gone. Bailey wriggled as if he sensed the urgency firing Cade's blood. He led the gelding into the paddock and swung onto his back.

Baying, the beagle pup raced out of the barn and darted toward the pasture gate. "Bailey!" Cade shouted, but the dog didn't stop. He ran full-tilt with his nose to the ground. "Atta boy, furball. Go get her," Cade said, kicking Dancer's flanks. The gelding bolted after the dog.

Into the mountains they went. Cade's heart pounded along with the gelding's hoofbeats. His breath strangled in his throat every time he imagined what must have happened to Allyson. Unable to see much in the gathering shadows, he followed the pale flicker of Bailey's tail tip. The dog led him on through denser and denser trees. Doubt washed through him. Would Bailey lead him to her, or was he on a fool's errand? What if he was already too late? *Please, please, let her be safe,* he prayed, clutching the reins.

The faint revving of a motor cut into the silence of the forest. When the trail widened out into a fork, Bailey streaked eastward, away from the noise. Torn with indecision, Cade stopped the gelding. Dancer snorted and sidestepped, fighting the bit. The west fork of the trail showed tire tracks in the dim light filtering down through the trees. Already, Bailey had disappeared into the woods.

Swearing, Kincade kicked the gelding into a canter toward the east. "I hope you're right, furball."

He searched and listened for the dog, afraid to call out lest the intruder hear and pursue them.

Bushes rustled. Bailey's shining tail reappeared. The dog circled once, twice, then whined, sniffing the ground. After a moment, he rushed on.

Cade followed, urging Dancer through a narrow gap in the trees. The horse took a handful of steps and stopped abruptly, tossing his head as they emerged into open space. They stood at the edge of a twenty-foot drop. "Good man," he said to the horse, patting its neck.

Bailey woofed and raced down into the gully and up the other side, finding his way easily in the brush. He spun in circles beside a tree with broken branches. Deep scuffmarks raked the leaf litter.

Cade rode Dancer along the gully's edge until he found a way to traverse it. When he reached the spot where the dog leaped in frantic figure-eights, he saw what had grabbed Bailey's attention. The small white object tore Cade's breath from his chest and drove shards of ice into his body.

Ally's shoe.

In the next instant he was galloping through the forest again, all thought of stealth gone. "Allyson! Answer me!" His call echoed through the woods and faded. Wild with fear, he pressed the gelding on. Sweat lathered the horse's neck.

The pup bayed once and rushed along the trail ahead of them, leaping fallen branches and dodging rocks. The gelding raced after him while Cade struggled to breathe.

Then Bailey lost the trail. Heartsick, Cade stopped his horse and watched the dog circle madly through the bracken. *Fool, you fool,* he cursed himself. *Whatever made you think anything mattered but her?*

The ringing of his cell phone pierced the mountain silence. Cade fumbled in his shirt pocket and clapped the phone to his ear. "Hello?"

"Kincade," came the staticky voice on the other end. Whatever else the caller said faded in and out.

"Who is this?"

"Brady, Brady Hart!" the caller roared, clear for a moment and then choppy again. "Listen—a problem—Riegel—cattle—dangerous..."

"Brady, I can't hear a damn thing. I'm up in the mountains. Ally's missing." Panic closed Cade's throat and his gaze locked on Bailey as the dog raced back and forth over his own tracks.

"...found some papers—bank's involved—he's crooked..."

Everything dropped into place. Paul Riegel, Maryanne's fiancé. A real estate broker. And the bank was involved. Paul had been trying to steal Hope Creek out from under Kincade and his family.

He might have killed Allyson already.

Cade's blood burst into flames. At least now, he had a face to pin his wrath on. "Thanks, Brady. I'll call you." He snapped the phone shut and shoved it in his pocket again.

Bailey circled a few more times, then went stiff as a statue with his tail in the air. Dancer snorted. Bailey gave a snarl and leaped into the shadows.

A man stumbled onto the trail. Paul, almost unrecognizable, his hair in leafy disarray and his clothing stained with dirt.

An inhuman growl erupted from Cade's throat. "Where is she?" He couldn't recognize his own voice.

"I'd like to know that myself," Paul said. The whites of his eyes flashed in the dim light spilling down through the trees. He raised a shaky arm, pointing a gun at Kincade. "Get down off that horse."

With a strength he didn't know he possessed, Cade sprang off the gelding's back and flew at Paul, throwing all of his weight behind the attack.

He collided with Paul just as the man fired the gun. The shot went wild. Bailey growled and leaped forward. Cade felt the man swing his foot. The dog yelped and tumbled away, but came roaring back with puppy-throated fury.

Cade swung his fist and connected with Paul's face in a satisfying crunch. He grabbed for the gun. Paul jammed an elbow in Cade's side. Pain smacked through Cade and he recoiled. Paul slipped around the dog and rushed for the gelding.

Cade threw his arms in the air toward the horse. "Ha! Ha!"

Dancer shied backward, tail lashing the air. Paul reached for the reins and missed. Cade shoved the horse back. The gelding spun in a nervous circle and Cade slapped his hindquarters. "Go!" he bellowed.

The gelding bolted forward and cantered out of sight. Out of Paul's reach. "You and me, now," Cade said. "You better hope to God she's alive, Riegel."

"Wouldn't know," the man said, his voice muffled by a broken and bleeding nose, "but I hope not. Hate to have her save your freakish hide."

Circling him, waiting for an opening, Cade said, "What are you talking about?"

"Whatever you are, you're gonna stay broken. And I'm gonna get this land for a song." Paul circled away.

"Maryanne," Cade guessed. She must have mentioned the town gossip about Cade's mysterious farming ability...but how could Paul believe it? Bailey ran to and fro around Cade's feet as he sidestepped, still growling.

"She doesn't know what the hell you are, either," spat Paul. "That airheaded little rich girl doesn't think beyond her next shopping trip. I did some guessing and took the rest on faith." He wiped his bloody nose on his shirtsleeve and pointed the gun again. "Nice to see I'm right."

The gunshot ripped the air. Pain tore through Cade's shoulder and flung him backward off his feet. He landed with a crushing thud and found himself gasping for air that wouldn't come.

Paul appeared above him, silhouetted by stars. "Hurts, eh? I've been shot before. Jealous husband." Mad-eyed, he laughed while the dog bayed into the night. Cade writhed on the ground, desperate for breath and half-blinded by agony. "Guess we'll never know if that redheaded bitch really fixes you," said Paul. "That kind of works for me." He pointed the gun again.

A piercing shriek rang through the forest, and a massive dark shape hurtled toward Paul. Through swamping pain, Cade recognized the whistle of an enraged horse. The animal struck at Paul, forcing him back, back, back into the trees. Dancer?

Air seeped into his lungs at last. He sucked in a huge, grateful breath and struggled to get his feet under him.

The horse was Diablo.

Paul gave up trying to aim his gun, swore, and fled into the trees. A few seconds later, Cade heard the sputtering of an engine that faded quickly into the distance.

Ally. Ally. Ally.

Ignoring the mind-rending pain in his shoulder, Cade slumped toward the stallion's big frame. Diablo gave an equine growl. His hide shivered. "Please," Cade whispered, unsure who he was pleading with. He heaved himself onto the stallion's back, awkward and unstable. Diablo crow-hopped, shaking his head and arching as if to buck. Cade gripped with his knees and clutched Diablo's mane with his good hand. "Easy, easy. It's me," he said.

Diablo snorted and fought for another few moments, and then sprang forward. Cade found himself on a breath-stealing gallop through the trees, dazed with pain and wondering if he were caught in some unimaginable nightmare.

Ally. Ally. Ally.

He steered the stallion toward Brady's land,

hoping Ally had escaped in that direction—God, he couldn't even consider the alternative. They galloped on for what felt like years. Fire raged in his shoulder.

At last, they burst into the open on a downhill slope, running into a gorge that backed up to Brady's land. Diablo skidded in a patch of loose gravel on his way down, jostling Cade's shoulder. Shooting pain blinded him. All he knew was the snorting of the horse and the tumbling of loose rocks. By the time they reached bottom, his strength had sapped to near nothing. "Ally," he called, the sound barely a whisper in his raw throat.

The stallion gave a nervous whicker. Cade squinted into the shadows as Diablo came to a dizzying stop.

"Cade!" For one beautiful moment, Allyson's voice chased away all thought of his pain. He half-slid, half-fell from the stallion's back and staggered toward the pale shape emerging from the darkness.

Her soft, sweet body collided with his. "Oh, God, you're bleeding. Cade, there's so much blood..." Tears choked her voice. Her hand came down over his shoulder, covering the wound, but the pressure forced a moan out through his lips.

"You're alive," he whispered, slumping against her. "That's all that matters." He let his forehead fall against the curve of her neck and breathed in her scent. With his good arm, he pulled her hard against him, memorizing her because he knew he'd never get this close again.

She trembled in his embrace. An ugly bruise marred her forehead. He pressed a gentle kiss over it. "Paul...is he gone?" she asked.

"No. You've got to get out of here. Take Diablo." His body shook with chills. His knees gave out and he collapsed.

"Cade! Cade!" Raw terror speared her voice and

she knelt beside him. One hand swept his hair back. The other pressed again on his shoulder as she tried to stop the flow of blood. "Oh, God, Cade, please—don't die, don't die. I love you, I love you..."

Some distant part of him burst with bittersweet joy even as agony twisted through his fire-and-ice body. "Don't say that—until you know the truth," he whispered.

Sobbing, she caressed his face. "What do you mean?"

He fought to sit up. Whatever else happened, he must confess everything. She deserved to know. If he told her and she reviled him, he would have to bear it—but he *would* tell her. He loved her too much to lie anymore. "I'm an earth Elemental," he said. "I could grow anything...once. It's gone now, reversed. This dying ranch... It's not your fault it can't be saved. It's me." He forced himself to look her in the eye, to show her he spoke the truth. Forced himself to admit his failure and live with it.

"You?" she said, almost to herself. "Then all my research, all my work... It was for nothing."

"No. No, Ally." He struggled against the ever-stronger call of unconsciousness and leaned closer to her, aching with more than the pain of his wound. "You have helped me get closer to saving Hope Creek than I thought possible. I wanted you to stay, wanted to fix this. But I can't do that to you. I can't use you, use *us*, like that. It meant too much." Molten-lava despair welled into every hollow of his being. He choked it back and waited for her condemnation. Even the pain of his shoulder couldn't compare to this anguish.

He saw the swift progression of thoughts across her features. The doubt, the caution, the way she connected events so that they led her in a perfect, straight line to the inevitable conclusion: he was an abomination and a stone-hearted manipulator. She had every right to take that horse and gallop out of his life.

The faint rev of an engine grew louder and louder, echoing off the rocky walls surrounding them. "Go!" Cade begged.

Her eyes flew wide. She snatched a large rock in each hand and lumbered to her feet, standing unsteadily on her injured ankle—but she didn't go.

Paul roared into the gorge on a four-wheeler whose headlights sliced into the darkness. Diablo bolted away into the deeper shadows.

Paul lurched off the vehicle and swayed toward them. "Oh, good, you're together," he said in a voice oozing with menace. "That makes this a lot easier."

With a howl of rage, Ally hurled one of her rocks at him. It thudded against Paul's chest. He stumbled back with an expression of amazed pain. Before he had the chance to recover, she flung the other rock. It slammed into the man's knee. Paul swore and rushed for her with his gun raised.

Not Ally not Ally not Ally not Ally. A siren-wail of fierce, desperate love resounded through Cade's body. He summoned everything he was and rolled to his knees. "No-o-o-o!"

****

Cade's scream tore Ally's horrorstruck attention away from the gun. He jammed the fingers of both his hands into the earth and gritted his teeth against what must have been maddening pain.

And he glowed.

First a shimmer at his fingers, then along his arms, over the curve of his back and down to his feet until a sun-bright aura surrounded him. The glow punched through the shadows and thrust the gorge into daylight.

The earth snarled under her feet. Gasping, she staggered backward, but the sound rushed away underground toward Paul. Shock drew the man's face into a taut, open-mouthed mask.

Vines speared upward through the rocky ground and exploded into the air. They ripped Paul off his feet. The man gave a terrified cry and Ally caught the flash of his gun spinning away through the air. A deafening rumble filled the gorge. Stones began to tumble down the mountainsides, then rocks, then boulders. One of them bashed against Paul and flung him against his all-terrain vehicle. He slumped into a heap and went still.

The rockslide subsided until only pebbles clattered along the slopes. Dust whooshed through the air and she coughed, holding her sleeve over her mouth and nose. "Cade?" she called, muffled, picking her way through the rubble toward him.

Kincade rocked back on his heels, shaking. His aura dimmed and died. He gave her one weary, heartbreaking look and passed out.

"Allyson?" a voice called from somewhere high above. "Kincade?"

Ally recognized Ethan's voice and pulled her hand away from her mouth. She reached Kincade and panic rocked her to her roots. "He's hurt! Come quick!"

Hoofbeats bounced off the walls of the gorge. Ethan, Brady, Morgan, and Elsa appeared from the direction of Brady's land. Rope in hand, Brady vaulted down from his saddle and trussed Paul like a wayward calf, swearing up a storm.

Cade's foster siblings materialized at Ally's side. Kneeling, Morgan surveyed Cade's injuries. "Oh, my God."

Elsa's gaze swept around the gorge. Her eyes filled with tears. "Morgan, he must have punched it."

"Are you nuts?" Ethan said, glaring down at Cade's still form. "Bleeding like that, and you force your power as high as it will go—" He broke off with a nervous look at Ally.

216

"I know. He did it for me," she said, surprising herself with how calm she sounded. Tears blinded her and poured down her cheeks. "Please, just get him out of here. He needs help."

Elsa brought Diablo, slipping a rope halter over his head. The stallion submitted, looking as drained as Ally felt.

She had no memory of how they returned to the ranch, nor any recollection of their trip to the hospital in Browning. A stream of people came to see Kincade, leaving flowers and cards and well wishes. Cade didn't wake up once. Heartsick, she stayed by his side and waited. At last, numb with exhaustion, she allowed Elsa to shepherd her back to the ranch. She fell asleep almost as soon as she got out of the truck.

She woke to filtered sunlight and the sight of a beautiful, hand-hewn cedar bedpost. Pushing into a sitting position, she spread her hands over the sturdy blue-denim comforter.

Kincade's room.

Something shifted at the end of the bed. A brown-and-black blur sprang at her. Bailey yipped, his tail whipping the air as he assaulted her with slobbery canine kisses. "Hi, sweetie," she said, scratching under her dog's chin. The pup bayed ecstatically.

A few moments later, the door swung open and Kincade appeared with his arm in a sling.

Heedless of her still-tender ankle, Allyson launched herself off the bed and into his arms.

He gave a soft grunt and wrapped his free arm around her. "I've been waiting for that for two days," he said into her hair. She heard him draw a deep breath with his nose pressed against her skin.

"Oh, Cade, I was so scared. I thought I'd never get to tell you..." She wiped away a rush of tears and looked into his deep green eyes.

"Tell me what?"

"It doesn't matter to me what you are. You're you, and I love you," she said. A ferocity of emotion bounded up inside her. She willed him to feel it.

Cade didn't speak. He didn't move. He simply gazed at her as if it were the only meaningful act in his life.

"Didn't you hear me?" she asked, hurt. "Didn't you say how much this meant?"

He seemed to thaw out from some frozen state. He hugged her hard, and when he spoke, his voice broke over the words. "Oh, Ally. I'll say it however you want. Whenever. I love you, I love you, I love you." He covered her with kisses. The tension that had been embedded in his body ever since they met eroded away, and he was there—her Kincade, blazing and passionate and loving her until she soared.

At last, he arched away and cupped her face in his warm, rough hand. "You gave me back everything I am," he whispered.

"And I love it all," she said back.

When they emerged into the kitchen with Bailey bouncing along at their heels, they met Cade's foster siblings around the kitchen table. Ethan pushed a hot cup of coffee toward her. "Welcome back. Your department called. I think Doctor Coonan dropped the word 'promotion' a few times." He smiled, but Ally caught a flash of unhappiness across Cade's features.

She devoured a muffin and two cups of coffee, during which they told her Paul was arrested and the bank's business locked in a scandalous legal battle. Hope Creek's deed would be safe for a long time. Time enough, she learned, for him to use his recovering gift to help the crops flourish and be ready for fall harvest.

"Cade, are you sure you can do this yourself?"

Elsa asked, her brow furrowed with worry.

"It's getting better every time I test it," he responded, holding up his good hand. "I'll be fine."

"What do you mean, himself? Aren't you going to be here?" wondered Ally.

"Cade's been taking care of us and putting it all on himself for too long," Morgan said. "That's pressure enough for anyone, but it wreaked havoc on his power."

Elsa gave a long, happy sigh and rested her chin in her hands. "And the way he feels about you brought it back."

"I guess it's about time we stopped tormenting him and got on with our lives," Ethan agreed. He grabbed another muffin and grinned at Morgan. "I am gonna miss your cooking."

"Me, too," Cade said with a laugh.

Morgan cleared the table and laid the dishes in the sink. "Go to Rose's diner. I've given her all my recipes."

"You're going to need extra hands while you're out in the fields, Cade," Ally said.

"I'll hire on. Brady knows some good men."

Indignant, she rounded on him. "And you know a good woman. Do you think I'm going back to Bozeman now? You need someone to watch over all those students when they come here for field projects. Julie can sit in some dusty little office. Not me."

One-armed, Cade hauled her into his lap. "I was hoping you'd say that, because I already ordered this and had it rushed." He pulled a small box from his pocket.

Each of his siblings started beaming. With a trembling hand, Ally opened the box. Inside lay a stunning diamond ring. Set in the gold band was a dark, flat-woven stripe that ran all the way around and under the shimmering stones at the top. "What's that?" she breathed.

"Strands of hair from Diablo's tail. They wove it right into the jewelry. I couldn't think of a more appropriate way to ask you to marry me, Allyson Hamilton."

Laughter turned to tears, and tears to sobs. "Yes, yes, oh, yes!" she cried, kissing him. Dimly she heard cheers and clapping from Cade's brother and sisters.

One by one, Cade's family drifted away and left the house. Even Bailey trotted into the living room to lie down. Cade kept kissing her back until she reeled with dreamlike bliss.

She remembered where she was only when he stood up and tugged her across the kitchen to his bedroom. "We have some catching up to do," he said. "I've got to make up for all those times I tried resisting you."

"Yes, you do, Kincade Murphy," she agreed, floating. And she followed him into his room knowing that finally, suddenly, all was right with the world.

A word about the author...

Nicki Greenwood grew up in suburbia, where there wasn't much room for a horse. Instead, she fed her equine obsession with the ink-and-paper kind. When she ran out of horse books to read, she wrote her own. Thus began her love affair with the written word, a passion that continues to this day.

At age thirteen, Nicki entered the National Spelling Bee and made third place runner-up in Central NY. She wrote stories and poetry for school publications and personal amusement throughout her youth. Eventually, she stumbled on the romance genre, and there she found her niche. Nicki loves blending an exciting adventure with an optimistic happy ending.

Nicki lives in upstate New York with her husband, son, and assorted pets. When she's not writing, she enjoys the arts, gardening, interior decorating, and trips to the local Renaissance Faire.

And The Black Stallion is still her hero.

Visit Nicki at: http://www.nickigreenwood.com

Thank you for purchasing
this Wild Rose Press publication.
For other wonderful stories of romance,
please visit our on-line bookstore at
www.thewildrosepress.com

For questions or more information
contact us at
info@thewildrosepress.com

The Wild Rose Press
www.TheWildRosePress.com

Other Faery Rose titles to enjoy:

THE SUMMONS by Jo Barrett
Was he real or had she lost her mind? Lindsay Sumner, an overworked nurse, isn't quite sure what to make of the handsome Highlander who is bound and determined to love her—all of her, body and soul.

THE DRAGON OF CROATIA by Valerie Everhart
Gavriel Dimitrios, the dragon of Croatia, is loose and with vengeance on his mind. Stubborn Callie Stewart, the woman responsible for his release from the ancient stone tablet, may be too cozy with the smugglers Gavriel has vowed to capture.

SOMEWHERE MY LOVE by Beth Trissel
Star-crossed lovers have a rare chance to reclaim the love cruelly denied them in the past, but can they grasp this brief window in time before it is too late?

COLOR OF DREAMS by Tia Dani
What happens when a Wiccan high-priestess and three mischievous nymphs conjure spells on an environmentalist and a jet engine designer? Could be magic, mayhem, and wild nights of passion.

KINGMAKER'S GOLD by M K Mancos
Gold—the word alone evokes dreams of riches beyond imagination. Whether one is a mortal woman or one of the fey men who inhabit New York in 1910, the precious metal can have great impact and far-reaching consequences.

ZORROC: FELINE PREDATORS OF GANZ, BOOK 1
by Lil Gibson
Legends, folklore, and science fiction all have a thread of truth as far as Catarina Achilles is concerned. One evening reality and fantasy merge to form a cat man she initially believes is a pooka. Before she can realize her blunder and divine his intentions, he steals her away to a world of deceit, betrayal...and fevered desire.